HER SHIFTER PACK

PERFECT SHIFTING PAIRS
BOOK FOUR

AMELIA SHAW

TAMSIN BAKER

CHAPTER 1

OLIVER

Being one-half of a "perfect pair" wasn't all it was cracked up to be.

For one thing, everyone liked my larger twin better. The girls fell all over Markus for his big, dumb muscles. They didn't care that I was the brains of the operation and always had been. Even in high school.

Women had been obsessed with my twin brother since we were young, and tonight was no exception.

"You heard from that girl you met the other night?" I called out to Markus, who was sitting across the table from me, making eyes at some woman nearby.

"Hey!" I shouted louder when he didn't respond, trying to raise my voice above the loud bass of the music. "Markus!"

My brother turned to me, narrowing his eyes. "What?"

I groaned. "Nothing. You… just go." I flicked my hand, indicating he should follow his instincts and go pick up whichever woman was giving him the right signals.

"But we're hanging out," Markus said, indicating between himself and me.

I drank the rest of my beer in a single swallow and got to my feet. "I'm heading home. You go do... her."

Markus chuckled as he stood up. "Bro, I—"

"I know. I know." I crossed the space between us and hugged my brother, older than me by a whole four minutes. "Go for it. I'm gonna head home."

"No, Ollie. Stay. There are a ton of hot chicks here tonight, and you haven't gone out with anyone since—"

"Forever. I know." I grinned at my mountain of a brother, though I suspected the grin was a little off-kilter given my mood. "I can't, Markus. I'm done." I held up my hands, feeling the all too familiar tug at my heart. I was finished screwing around.

It had been fun for a while. But we'd turned thirty a few months ago, and I was done with this life. I was ready to settle down. I wanted a mate and a family.

Markus wasn't done, and that was fine. Except... it wasn't. Not when he was the other half of our perfect pair. His actions were affecting me in a way normal men wouldn't understand. As a pair, we were bound to each other.

Past. Present. And more importantly, future.

I took a step toward the door, the desire to take another jab at a very touchy subject passing over me. "Can you hurry up and get this out of your system so we can find our mate?"

Markus growled at me. "I don't believe in that perfect pair shit. You know that."

I laughed at his petulant expression, though the sound was laced with bitterness. "You're one of a perfect pair, Mark. It doesn't matter if you believe it or not. Fate believes in it for you, and there's nothing you can do to change that."

I turned away before the heat of my brother's glare lit my hair on fire.

I left the bar, passing by the bouncers letting people in two at a time. It was midnight, and the night was only just starting. I was tired of it. The scene, the fake smiles, the surface-only care; all of it.

Being a perfect pair meant far more than people knew. Markus and I were like a perfect man, split into two. We were both good-looking if the women we'd dated were to be believed. But while I got the brains, Markus got the brawn. He was a clown, and I could be too serious. Together, we balanced each other out.

Something neither of us had counted on, though, was that perfect pairs were expected to share a mate. According to shifter lore, there was one Fated mate out there for each perfect pair. One woman created just for us. The only problem with that concept, was that my brother didn't want a mate. Or a wife. Or a family.

Fuckwit.

I patted the pockets of my jeans, and groaned. "Damn it." Markus had the car keys.

My gaze drifted across the road, where more bars and restaurants were filling with people, clashing styles of music pumping out of every speaker to create a cacophony of noise.

My wolf shifter senses enhanced the world around me. The intense sound of the cars, the people, and the music, were even more garish in my shifter ears than they would have been for a human. The multi-layered scents were heightened, too. Pungent, horrible aftershave and too strong perfume. Whiskey and stale beer. Fried, greasy food layered beneath sweat and body odor.

Not the sort of environment my shifter craved. He desired fresh grass, tall trees and the space to roam free.

My wolf prowled just beneath the surface of my skin, agitated and alone. I needed to shift and run, but there was no space for that here in the city. No freedom to be myself.

We lived in a small city with humans everywhere. My pack elders, many generations ago, had chosen to be part of humanity. We all had normal jobs; normal lives. We pretended to be human most of the time.

But our instincts were all wolf. Our strength. Our speed. Our wives... Fated mates. There were some things we just couldn't get away from, even if we tried.

I shoved my hands into my pockets and began to walk along the sidewalk. Home was only about five miles, and once I was out of the city blocks, I could run. Not in wolf form, but at least I could get up a sweat and work off some of the anger pushing through my veins.

I stopped at a walkway, looking each way for traffic, and then when there was a gap, I hurried across the street.

My heart hurt in a way that it never used to. Like there was a hole in the flesh around it. Like someone had been trying to gouge it out.

Like there was something wrong with me.

Markus said he didn't feel what I did. The bone-deep, cold loneliness that had begun to infiltrate my heart years ago and had built to unbearable proportions now. He was happy to continue playing around. We were only thirty, he said. And in one sense he was right. We still had time to find our Fated mate.

But I wasn't sure how much longer I could put up with this aching loneliness.

Alexandria

My mom had been a biker chick, but that wasn't the life I wanted to lead. So, at eighteen and one day, I'd packed my things and headed off to create a new life for myself. Far away from my mother's world.

Who knew that life on the outside could be more difficult than the upbringing I'd had?

"Hey! You!"

I grimaced at the angry male voice yelling at me from across the diner. He hadn't technically said my name but, even without looking, I was pretty sure he was calling to me. It was midnight on a Saturday night, and we were far busier than usual.

I turned around and pressed a hand to my chest. "Me, sir?"

His brows drew together as he glared at me like an angry bear with a sore paw. "Yes, you. Get your fat ass over here."

The gasps around the diner were louder than any shout. People were clearly appalled at his behavior, but I knew no one would stand up for me. They never did.

My cheeks burning, I tried to suck in my stomach as much as I could and hurried across the linoleum floor, pen in hand. "Can I help you, sir?"

Embarrassment mixed with anger in my gut, making my stomach churn and my teeth clench. But I held tight to that boiling pot and breathed through the feeling.

My boss, like so many others, ascribed to the motto that the customer was always right. I, however, did not agree. Not in every case. And the temper I'd inherited from my long-gone father had way too short a fuse.

But I had bills to pay, so I didn't have much of a choice at this point, except to suck it up and get the job done.

"Yeah, you can take my order," the red-haired bear growled at me. "I've been waiting for a fucking hour."

My lips twisted as I stared down at the black pencil tip poised on the paper. He'd barely been here ten minutes. I'd seen him come in. Whereas I'd been serving two dozen people on my own for several hours, since Nancy had called in sick last minute.

Not to mention the fact that table seven had a two-year-old in a highchair who kept throwing food on the floor. The food was a slipping hazard so I had to keep stopping to clear it up. Poor thing was utterly exhausted and beyond cranky—and no wonder being midnight. My patience was growing thin with him too, or at least, with his parents who did nothing to help clean up their child's mess.

"What would you like, sir?" I asked through gritted teeth.

He grunted out his order full of grease and fat, just like him.

I jotted it down and turned to walk away. His hand slapped my ass so hard I yelped and fell forward.

I didn't mean to punch him, but I'd swung around and my arm shot out before I could think fast enough to stop it.

A general round of applause went up in the room as he fell sideways in his booth.

I gasped and pressed my fist to my lips, blowing on the aching knuckles. "Shit."

"Lexie! What the hell have you done?" My boss stood in the kitchen serving area, staring wide-eyed at the scene.

I sprinted for the counter and rounded the wooden bench. "Oh, shit."

"You stupid girl!" he yelled, as he ran from the kitchen and into the dining area.

I didn't stop to ask about my last two weeks' pay, I just grabbed my bag and ran for the exit. My damn temper always got me in trouble. This wasn't the first job I'd lost because I'd struck a customer who tried to manhandle me, and it probably wouldn't be the last.

I pushed open the glass door, the bells tinkling above my head. When I glanced back, I saw my boss lifting the guy back to a seated position, his angry gaze landing on me.

He lifted his arm and flicked his hand. "Get out of here. And don't you ever show your face here again."

I groaned as I rushed out the door and straight into the chest of a man mountain. "Holy shit. I'm so sorry." Then I looked up into the most beautiful blue eyes I'd ever seen.

I stumbled back, gaping at his gorgeous face. My heart pounded in my chest just looking at him.

He reached out for me, grabbing my arms to steady me. "Whoa there, you okay?"

A frisson of electricity sizzled through my body like I'd touched an electrified fence.

I shivered at the feeling, liking it and yet finding it strangely uncomfortable all at the same time.

His reaction was a lot more intense than mine. He staggered sideways, reaching out for the glass window to my left to steady himself.

"Hey, Ollie, you all right?" A deep, sexy voice called out from further down the street.

Another man headed toward us, even more handsome than the

first, if that was possible. But he was different to the man I'd run into. Bigger. Broader. Dark, where the first man was light.

"I didn't mean to hurt him. He just..." I was about to explain to the second man that the first one had zapped me, but the door to the diner flung open and the big bear that I'd punched stood in the doorway glaring at me.

The left side of his face was red and swelling. "Get back here!"

I didn't stop to find out what he wanted from me. Would he punch me back? Call the cops? Haul me down to the police station himself? Probably.

Shit!

I had to go. But, as I took a step back, my heart called out to stay. To speak to the two men staring at me as though they'd never seen a woman before.

Fear won out, and the adrenaline pumping through my veins had me turning away from all the men who were staring at me and running down the street.

"Just go. Keep going, and don't look back," I chanted to myself, my feet beating against the pavement in time with the rapid tattoo of my heart.

CHAPTER 2

MARKUS

My brother was shaking. I had no idea why, but it had something to do with that girl.

The one who was currently running away from us down the street. Her big ass and huge boobs shook as she ran. Not my usual type, but damn, did I enjoy watching her hurry away.

I couldn't seem to drag my eyes away from her, and my wolf was prowling uncomfortably inside my chest, wanting to shift. Wanting to run after her.

But why?

I forced myself to focus back on my brother, mentally shaking myself. I'd never wanted to run after a woman before in my life. They chased me, not the other way around.

"Hey. Are you okay?" I reach for Ollie's arm, not liking how pale his face was.

He pushed up to standing, though he still swayed like he was intoxicated. "Yeah. Fine. I just... where'd she go?"

He was looking around as though he expected the hot chick to reappear.

I shrugged. "She ran off."

"Did you see which way she went?" a guy asked, stepping toward us.

He had a terrible vibe about him. Almost like he was a bear shifter, but darker than they usually were.

I turned toward the red-bearded giant. "What do you want with her?"

"Fucking bitch punched me in the jaw," he said, leaning forward to spit blood on the sidewalk. "Knocked a tooth loose."

She's tough, then. Good. I wasn't sure why that would matter, but pleasure ran through me at the thought of her standing up for herself —as I'm sure she'd just had to, judging by this guy's angry demeanor.

I couldn't help but ask, "Whatcha do to deserve that?"

He glared at me, and I just grinned back. Let him make a move. I wouldn't mind a fight tonight. But the coward just turned and marched back inside the diner.

Ollie was slowly but surely moving his way forward, dragging his legs.

"Ollie! Wait up." I jogged to catch up to him. "What happened to you back there?"

He was getting stronger, straightening his spine and walking more upright now. "That girl you let go. She's our mate."

I put my hand out to stop him, grabbing on tighter when he wanted to keep moving. "Wait. Say that again?"

Ollie turned to me, his cheeks slashed with heat. "She's our mate, Markus. I've never felt anything like it. One touch of her skin against mine, and she took my legs out from under me."

"But—"

"But what?" he asked, twisting his body and tugging his arm out of my grip.

How could I tell my brother the truth? That I didn't want a mate, period, let alone one I had to share. What was the point of having one woman who was everything I could ever want in a wife, only to have to share her with my brother?

When I didn't respond, Ollie kept moving. "I'm going to look for her." He sniffed the air, turned left, then took off running up the street.

I groaned and ran a frazzled hand through my hair. "Ollie... shit..." I turned back the way I'd come. I'd been at the bar, about to buy a drink for a woman dripping with lust, but I'd had an urge to leave her and go find my brother.

Stupid move. Stupid, stupid move.

But even now, with the knowledge that if I bolted back to the bar, the same woman would be there waiting for me with a hot smile and an even hotter body, I couldn't do it.

I had to stay with Ollie. Every instinct in my gut told me not to abandon my brother at this moment.

I took off at a run, catching up with him a block down. "Wait up!"

Ollie didn't slow down, but I could tell he heard me. He was sniffing the air, following a scent.

"Can you sense her?" I asked, getting ready to shift and run despite the city environment. We would hunt her down and demand to know who she was. Surely, she'd be a shifter too. Maybe a woman from a pack outside the city?

I'd never seen her before. Not at a city pack gathering, nor any of the full moon parties we'd attended. We would have definitely noticed her. She was seriously hot.

Ollie dropped his chin and stared straight at me. "No. I think she's gone."

"Gone?" I repeated. "She can't just disappear."

My brother's eyebrows drew together. "She was running away from that guy at the diner. She was scared."

"So, she's hiding?" I scoffed. "Not likely. That chick was tough! And probably a shifter too, if you think she's your mate. What human would punch a guy that big?"

Ollie stared at me like I'd gone crazy, his eyes as round as the moon.

"What?" I demanded, unable to ignore the way his expression flared with anger.

"She's not a shifter, Mark. She's a human, and she's afraid. And she's *our* mate, not just mine. How many times can you be fucking wrong in the same sentence?"

The fury I kept a lid on most of the time began to boil inside me. "Hey. Back off. I followed you because I felt bad you left and wanted to keep you company. I could be on my way home with some woman, but instead I'm here listening to you bitch and moan."

Ollie stepped closer until we were practically nose to nose. He was a few inches shorter than me, but it didn't stop him from glaring straight into my eyes.

"Fuck off, Markus. I mean it. Go! You wanna be balls deep in some stranger's pussy every night of the week, then do it. I don't give a shit anymore."

Then he walked away.

I gaped as I watched him go, then yelled out, "You say that like it's a bad thing!"

Dickhead.

I turned in the opposite direction to Ollie and marched back toward the bar. Who the hell was he to judge me? Men didn't do that to each other.

My friends honestly didn't give a shit if I was married or single. Fucking my way through the entire town or celibate. That wasn't what we judged each other on.

But Ollie and this stupid fucking perfect pairs bullshit...

A growl rolled through my chest and my hands clenched into tight fists. "Damn it... grr..." I forced my legs to walk faster.

I didn't want to settle down. I didn't want a mate. Hell, I wasn't sure I even wanted kids. Every time I heard one of them cry or saw a pregnant woman, I shuddered.

That just wasn't the life for me. I was sure of it.

I froze mid-stride, the sweetest scent I'd ever smelled filling my nose and teasing my senses. "What the..."

I looked around, searching for the source of the deliciousness. A couple walked by, and I sniffed loudly.

The guy shot me a look, and I shook my head and moved in the opposite direction. It wasn't them.

There was an alleyway between the two shops on the street, and I put my nose up and scented the air once more.

An involuntary groan rose from my chest when another erotic cloud of need hit me. "What the hell *is* that?"

I stalked down the dark alleyway, looking for the thing that was making all my senses go haywire. My wolf was on full alert, and it was only because of years of training that my human self was strong enough to subdue him.

I took another step, then another, part of me expecting to find some secret bakery hidden down here among the trash cans and piss puddles.

I sniffed again and managed to stifle the groan this time. It was stronger suddenly. Why could I sense... "You!"

To my left was the woman we'd seen running out of the diner. She was standing totally still, her back pressed against the concrete wall. If I didn't have wolf senses, which included night vision, I would never have seen her.

Her hands curled into fists and her huge breasts rose and fell as she began to pant, obviously readying for a fight.

And yet the words that came out of her pretty mouth were, "Please don't hurt me."

I turned to look right at her. What a contradiction this woman was. She seemed as tough as nails, and yet there was an insanely intoxicating amount of sweetness about her too.

I leaned forward a little and sniffed the air. "Why do you smell like cookies? Is it your perfume?"

It was a long shot, but I had to ask. My cock was thickening by the second, and if I didn't pride myself on always waiting for the woman to make the first move, I would have pushed her up against that wall and kissed her.

Her lips parted on a soft gasp. "Cookies? I..."

My question must have caught her off guard because her fingers unclenched from their fisted position, then she did something so strangely innocent and weird. She lifted her arm and sniffed at her armpit.

O... kay.

Then she dropped her arm again, a wince on her face. "Oh, I definitely don't smell of cookies. I've been working since six a.m., so all I can smell is sweat."

I leaned even closer. "I don't understand."

"Hey," she said, pointing her finger at me. "Didn't I see you before with that guy that kinda keeled over sideways? Is he okay?"

I chuckled for a moment then could almost hear Ollie in my head whispering, *"Touch her. Then you'll know."*

I didn't want to know whether she was my supposed mate or not. I chose my fate, not anyone else. But my wolf was howling at me to get closer, and I didn't like to see such a beautiful woman pressed into the dirt of the alley.

"He's fine. Gone home," I said with a shrug, swallowing the lump in my throat. "Come on, I'll give you a lift."

She shook her head. "No. I'm fine."

I gestured for her to follow me. "Well, I'm not leaving you in this alley. So, either tell me where you're staying, and I'll get you there or..."

She stared down at her hands, inspecting her unpolished nails. "Or what?"

I knew I should walk away. That this—whatever I was doing right now—was crazy.

I'd followed my wolf instincts into this alley and was now about to do the most stupid thing I'd done in a long time. "Or I'll take you home with me."

Her head shot up and her eyes were as round and wide as a startled deer.

I held both hands up. "Hey, this isn't a line. We have a spare bedroom. You can take Kaity's room."

"Who's Kaity?"

"Our baby sister. She visits on occasion." I stared at her long and hard, assessing her defeated posture and adding it to the list of questions I had. "You don't have anywhere to go, do you?"

She bit her lip in the most innocently seductive way, and I almost threw my head back and howled.

I forced myself to stumble further away from her, pushing down my wolf with all my might. "What is it about you?" I grumbled, putting a hand against the opposite wall to where she leaned, and breathing hard.

"What do you mean?"

I couldn't explain it, so I shook my head. She was already freaked out enough. I didn't need to tell her that every look made my senses overload.

When I could finally get myself under control, I stood straight and tugged at my shirt to straighten everything once more.

Unfortunately, I couldn't help but notice the way her gaze slid over me, and she didn't look repulsed. Quite the opposite. Even in the dim light I could see her pupils dilate.

"Come on... ah, I don't even know your name."

"It's Alexandria," she said. "But everyone calls me Lexi."

I crossed my arms over my chest to stop from reaching out for her. "What do you prefer?"

She tilted her head and frowned at me like no one had ever asked her that before. "Lexi."

"Done." *Sexy Lexy.* "Come on. Let's get out of here. Do you have a bag, or anywhere you've got some stuff stored?"

She nodded. "Sort of. I've been renting a loft over a Chinese restaurant on Castle Street, but my landlord is expecting my rent, and since I just lost my job and my boss didn't give me the last two weeks' pay he owed me, I'm kinda stuck."

She certainly was.

I held up a hand. "Hang on a second. Are you telling me that your old boss is holding your money?" My anger began to build. I hated men like that. Using their power and influence to keep those under them captive. How was she supposed to eat? Live? "How often is he supposed to pay you?"

"Weekly. But he's been a bit less forthcoming in recent weeks." She bit her lip again. I had to turn and walk away, toward the entrance of the alley, to stop from pulling her into my arms and drowning her in kisses.

What was wrong with me? This chick was not my usual type at all. She wasn't skinny and overtly sexual, and she damn sure wouldn't be an easy to forget one-night stand.

So why did I want to take her home, put her to bed, and devour her whole?

When I noticed she wasn't following me, I turned around and saw that she was still hanging around the trash cans.

I sighed. "Come on, Lexi. It's late. You're exhausted, and I'm frustrated as fuck. Let's just go home and get some sleep, and tomorrow, we can sort out your boss and your money."

She hurried up to me. "No. I don't want you doing anything to him."

I bit back my reply and instead just forced a smile to my face. "My truck's parked a few blocks over. You can take the spare bedroom tonight, okay?"

She narrowed her eyes at me as though assessing my intent.

I put both hands up in surrender. "Hey, don't look at me like that. I don't do unwilling women. And Ollie wouldn't harm a fly."

Her eyebrows flickered up. "Ollie... that's the guy from before?"

Jealousy like nothing else I've ever felt shot through me, hot and angry and uncomfortable.

"Yeah," I managed to get out through clenched teeth. "He's my brother."

It was almost strange to explain to someone who Ollie was. Everyone knew us. We'd lived here our whole lives.

She inhaled sharply, then nodded once. "Thank you. I accept your offer, and I hope I'll be able to pay you back sometime in the future."

I shrugged and shoved my hands in my pockets so I didn't reach for her. "Don't sweat it. You don't owe us anything."

I couldn't believe I was taking her home to sleep under our roof. It was like bringing meth into a halfway house. How were we going to survive?

"Your truck is... where?" she asked when we emerged from the dark alley.

"A few blocks over," I said, nodding in the direction of the club. "Not far from your diner, actually. Maybe we should pop in tonight and demand your wages?"

She shook her head adamantly. "No. Please don't."

"Okay," I agreed, but only because I wanted to come back at a non-peak time. Saturday night wasn't exactly quiet.

On a Tuesday morning there would be no one around to see me throttle the guy for taking advantage of her.

"This way?" she asked, pointing down the street.

"Yep."

We began walking and part of me desperately wanted to touch her, but the fear of what I'd feel if I did, stopped me.

She walked ahead while I stayed close behind her. She held

tightly to her shoulder bag, flinching as people came anywhere near touching her. "Which street?"

"Thomas Road," I said, and she hurried ahead, turning left into the correct street.

When I caught up with her, she was standing by my new black truck. "This one?" she asked, indicating the truck with her thumb.

I nodded, not even wanting to know how she'd guessed. There were several other trucks parked nearby.

"Yep," I said, the door locks opening as I stepped close enough with the key in my pocket to engage the fob. "Hop in."

She did, still clinging to her bag.

Once we put our seat belts on and I turned on the heater, she reached up and pulled the hair tie from the bun that had contained her hair.

I did not expect to see such glorious locks cascade down over her shoulders and halfway down her back. Dark rivers of softness with natural highlights that picked up every wave and curl.

I thanked everything that was holy that I hadn't yet started the truck. I might have driven straight off the road into a building.

"You okay?" she asked, glancing sideways at me as if sensing my shock. I must have been staring.

Shit. Get it together, idiot.

"Yeah. Yeah. Cool. Let's go." I turned the ignition on, planted my foot on the gas, then drove home.

I didn't speak most of the way. Instead, I spent most of the drive struggling to force my wolf back inside my tightly guarded control.

We pulled up outside the two-story house my brother and I had bought ten years ago. Ollie was standing on the front porch, reaching for the spare key above the door frame.

"Hey," he called out. "Sorry about before. I was being a dick."

I snorted. "Nothing new there." I hauled myself out of the truck, looking forward to his reaction. I stared at Ollie's face as his lips turned from a smirk into a gasp. His gaze focused on the woman behind me.

I tried to play it cool, though Ollie was not relaxed in the slight-est. "Lexi, here, needs a place to stay for the night," I said. "I offered her Kaity's room."

Ollie's gaze bounced from me to Lexi, and back again. "You... What.... How?"

I shook my head. "We'll catch you up inside. Let's get out of the cold."

I jogged up the steps, unlocked the front door and walked inside.

Inside was marginally warmer than outside, but not by much. Normally, that suited Ollie and me just fine. As wolf shifters, we ran hot. At least three degrees warmer than a human.

Lexie was going to freeze.

I went straight to the thermostat and cranked it up, taking off my jacket, which was mostly for show anyway. The best way to spot a wolf shifter in town was in the middle of winter, when we were all strolling around in t-shirts with not a care in the world about the icy weather around us.

The furnace fired into gear, groaning at the strain.

"Come in, come in," I heard Ollie call jovially from the front door.

There was a note of excitement in his tone, and once again that hot shot of jealousy had my gut churning. I needed to calm down and get a grip on this situation.

I walked toward the kitchen and turned back to call out, "You want a hot drink? Or a beer?"

Lexie stepped into the lounge room, the sweet smell of her filling my senses and making my knees weak. I grabbed for the door frame with one hand and locked my knees so I didn't stumble.

Get it together.

"A hot drink would be lovely," she said, her eyes wide as she stared around the room then back to me. "Hot chocolate? Pepper-mint tea? Anything really, just no caffeine. I'm already wired from too much coffee today."

She smiled and if I hadn't known it already, that was a sure sign I was in trouble. The way her eyes lit up and her lips curved... I'd never seen anyone so beautiful. My heart stuttered, taking my breath for a moment.

"Be back soon," I mumbled as I tore away from the door frame and forced myself into the kitchen.

I was an idiot. What on earth had possessed me to bring her back here? I shook my head as I walked over to the fridge for the milk, mumbling. "You dumb mother—"

"Hey, Markus, are you okay?"

Her voice was just so damn sweet. She had no right to sound that good.

"Yeah. No problem," I said, not turning around to face her, but instead opening the fridge and perusing the contents with thoroughness—as if I didn't know exactly what was inside.

"You seem on edge. If you want me to leave, I can."

I pressed my knuckles to my forehead, not sure which way to turn. Anxiety ate at me like a disease, making me want to run, hide, and fight, all at once.

"I've just got a bit of a headache. Nothing some sleep won't fix."

She quietened, so I went about making her a hot chocolate, our sister's favorite also, and opened a beer for myself.

Ollie came into the room and pulled out a beer for himself. "How did you find her, Mark?" he asked me quietly.

I didn't want to admit I followed her delicious scent, as if I couldn't help myself. I took a sip of my beer and stirred the chocolate mixture into the heated milk. "She was hiding in an alleyway, with nowhere to go. I couldn't leave her there."

Silence filled the room and when I turned around, Lexie was sitting at the table next to Ollie.

I placed her hot chocolate down in front of her, careful not to touch her hand as she reached for the large mug.

"Thank you so much," she said, wrapping her hands around the heated mug. "I can't remember the last time someone made me a drink."

I bit my tongue and leaned back against the kitchen counter, crossing my arms over my chest. Nope. I wasn't commenting or asking any more questions.

"So what happened with that jerk at the diner?" Ollie asked. "He said you hit him or something."

I dragged my gaze up in time to see a heated blush spread across Lexi's face.

I bit the inside of my cheek and stared at the floor once more.

How was it possible that everything she did was so damn cute? Even her blush tightened my jeans as my cock swelled in its confines.

"Oh, yeah. Well, I didn't mean to hit him, but he was harassing me and hit my ass, and I just... reacted."

I snorted out a laugh. "Sounds like he deserved it."

I looked at her briefly, unable to help myself. Her little smile made my stomach ache, so I attempted to ignore her again by looking down. The floor could do with a mop, I thought, trying to distract my brain—and my dick—from her delicious allure.

Ollie wasn't ignoring her; he was babbling out questions I already knew the answer to. "And what happened to your apartment or house? Not that I mind you staying here, but if we can help you out, we will."

"Oh, well..." Lexie launched into the story about her money and rent, and I grabbed my beer again, clinging to the ice-cold lifeline.

Maybe I could go back to the bar? Pick up that girl and bring her home. Surely, that would be enough to satisfy this hunger clawing at my gut. But the thought of doing anything with another woman while Lexie was under the same roof seemed... *wrong*. Maybe I could pick up the woman and go to hers? Or a hotel?

My stomach churned at the thought.

"Well, we'll help sort that out for you tomorrow," Ollie was saying. "Right, Mark?"

I nodded, then tipped back my head and skolled the rest of my drink. "Yep." That diner owner was gonna get a fist to the jaw if he didn't have a damn good reason for not paying Lexi.

She yawned suddenly, and Ollie hopped to his feet like a lapdog, eager to please. "Come this way, Lexi, I'll show you to your room."

She smiled at him as she got to her feet. "Thank you. That would be great. I can't believe an hour ago I was trying to work out where I might be able to find a bed, and now I'm here."

I couldn't help but ask, "Where *were* you planning on sleeping if I hadn't found you?"

She leveled me with the seriousness in her eyes. "Well, there's a few twenty-four-hour diners in the city that let you stay through the night if you order a coffee or two. Then there's the movie theater. The security guards rarely lock the back doors, so I've stayed a night or two in there. Or—"

"You what?" Ollie asked, horror filling his face.

I was just as shocked at her revelation, but tried to school my features so it didn't show.

She reached down for her mug and took another sip of her hot chocolate. "It's okay. There are a lot of places to safely sleep if you need to."

It's not okay, I thought. She shouldn't have to scrounge the city to find a safe place to sleep.

"But—" Ollie began, but I pushed myself off the counter and cut him off.

"Weren't you going to show her bedroom, Ollie? She's obviously exhausted."

Ollie stared at me for several seconds, his brow furrowed, then he seemed to understand that I meant for him to abandon his line of questioning.

"You're right. This way." He swept his arm out in a theatrical gesture toward the stairs.

I stayed where I was. I wasn't going to risk going anywhere near her tonight. She was temptation on a popsicle stick.

Lexie put her hand on Ollie's arm, and he shivered but didn't fall the way he had before. "Hang on one second."

She made her way over to me and my heart began to thump, worry and desire coursing through me in equal parts.

"What's up?" I asked, realizing I was trapped. The kitchen counter and cabinets were at my back, and she was right in front of me.

"I just wanted to say thank you. You don't know me at all, and you're trusting me, here, in your home. So... yeah, thanks."

I nodded, trying not to breathe at all. I didn't want to smell her again. She was too delectable.

"Okay... Well... good night." She stuck out her hand for me to shake.

Oh, God.

"It's all good," I said, not moving.

"Oh, okay," she said, her face falling, showing her disappointment.

I'd offended her. Crap!

I stuck my arm out. What was the worst that could happen? I didn't believe in the perfect pair Fated mate thing, so surely, I wouldn't be affected the way Ollie had been? "Sorry. Good night, Lexi."

She reached out and took my proffered hand, her beautiful eyes lighting up at my turnaround.

But her touch... Blow me down with a feather. From the moment her hand connected with mine, an electrical impulse shot through my system like I'd touched a wired-up fence.

I gasped and lost the battle of staying upright. The first thing I did was let go of her hand, but that didn't stop the effect. I staggered sideways, stumbling for something to hold on to.

There was nothing to grab, so I bit the dust, hard, hearing Ollie's cackle of a laugh mocking me from above.

Motherfucker...

CHAPTER 4

LEXI

I covered my mouth with my hand and stared down at the man mountain who'd just crumpled before my very eyes. "Oh my God, Markus! What happened?"

Ollie was laughing like a loon, barely standing on his feet himself, so I whacked him in the chest with my fist, trying to make him stop. "Hey! He could be hurt."

"Oh, he's not hurt," Ollie said, still chuckling. "Well, his pride might have taken a bit of a hit, but that's about it."

Markus was shaking himself and slowly getting to his feet.

I rushed forward. "Let me help you."

He practically cartwheeled away from me. "No! I'm fine. I'm fine."

He wasn't, but it was obvious he didn't want any help from me. It was as if he hated my touch. "Oh... yes... okay."

Ollie threw his arm around my shoulders in a brotherly-type move. Only, the embrace felt far from brotherly. I swallowed at the sudden flutter in my belly, trying to tamp down the feeling. "Come on, Lexi. Leave the baby to his sulking. I'll show you where you can sleep tonight."

I didn't want to leave Markus just standing there, shaking his head and staring down at the floor he'd just dragged himself up from, but Ollie steered me toward the stairs. "Come on. The bedrooms are on the top floor."

"Yours as well?" I asked, gulping as the reality of this situation suddenly hit me. What had I done? I'd accepted a ride from a stranger, and was now in their house, without anyone knowing where I was.

I knew better than this. I was probably safer in a booth at a diner, or alone in the cold, dark movie theater than I was in a house with two men I didn't know.

What if they'd drugged the hot chocolate? If they attacked me, or worse... what was I going to do? Or say? That I went home with them, climbed into one of their beds, but didn't want them? No one would believe me.

And, to be honest, my body was still fluttering with strange feelings that I couldn't understand. The electricity when I touched both of them freaked me out a little. But it had woken up my long-dormant sexy bits, and I didn't know what to do about that.

It was so inappropriate to be attracted to these two amazing men. Not one, but *both* of them, seemed to set off my inner "*yes please*" goddess in a way I couldn't remember ever happening before.

"Are you sure about this?" I asked as we walked slowly up the stairs. "You know I didn't come home with your brother to get into bed with either of you?"

Ollie laughed and removed his arm from my shoulders. "You don't have to worry, Lexi. We were taught to behave better than that. Our mother would quite literally skin us alive if we ever raised a hand to hurt a woman."

After years of living with liars and manipulators, I could spot bullshit a mile away. Ollie wasn't lying, and Markus hadn't been either when he'd offered me a safe place to stay. That sense of "rightness" was the reason I was here now.

"This is it," Ollie said, stopping and indicating a dark room.

He reached inside and flicked on the light. "It's a bit girly. Kaity decorated it when she was like... sixteen."

I stuck my head inside and smiled. The room's décor was mostly pink, with white and gold as contrasting colors. Definitely a teen vibe, rather than a grown woman. "It's really pretty."

"Sheets are clean," he said, as I slowly made my way into the room. "Bathroom is down the hall. I'll grab you a towel and leave it in there for you. I promise that no one will disturb you tonight. You're safe here."

He put his hand on his heart as though he was declaring a solemn oath.

I couldn't explain why, but I believed him. And his brother. I nodded and walked into the pretty pink room, then set my handbag down on the bed. "I won't be long. I'll just freshen up, and then go to bed."

Ollie frowned. "Do you need a shirt or something to sleep in?"

I glanced down at my soiled waitress uniform and grimaced. "Ah, yeah. I guess I do. I didn't pack my pajamas to go to work."

A slow, sexy smile spread across Ollie's face. "You weren't expecting a sleepover tonight?"

I snorted, trying to hide the lurch of my heart at that look on his face. I couldn't decide which of the brothers was sexier. They both seemed different, but it didn't matter to my lady bits.

"Hardly," I managed, after a pause. "I was supposed to be doing the six a.m. 'til six p.m. shift, but someone called in sick so I stayed on to help. I have a spare change of clothes in my bag only because I thought I might need to change to get home."

It was only a pair of jeans and a t-shirt, but at least they were clean, and I could wear them tomorrow.

"Give me a second," Ollie said, then ducked away.

I kicked my shoes off my aching feet and peeled my socks off. My sigh of relief filled the room as I sank my toes into the plush carpet. I shouldn't be here, and yet, it was such a sweet gift. Just one night of luxury. A warm, safe, clean bed in a real house.

I wasn't sure I'd ever had that before now.

"Here you go," Ollie said from the doorway, tossing a flannel shirt and a white towel onto the bed. "I don't wear that one a lot. I get too hot in it. So, you can keep it if you like."

I reached for the thick, warm material and brought it up to my face. "Thank you."

I tried not to be obvious about the fact that I was sniffing the shirt, but damn, it was so tempting. His scent, and that of Markus, was so enticing. I'd never noticed men smelling so damn good before.

"Good night, Lexi," Ollie said, his voice deep and husky as he waved at me and then disappeared from view.

I took a big sniff and groaned at how delicious the shirt smelled. Ollie had a very masculine scent, like hazelnuts and sweet sweat.

While Markus... I shivered even thinking about the big brother who'd hit the deck only minutes ago. What on earth had that been about? And could I handle the truth if I had the guts to ask the question?

My hand reached for the soft, fluffy towel. I would love a shower, but how safe would I be in their bathroom, naked and vulnerable?

I snorted out a laugh. Those two men were strong enough to pin me down and do anything they wanted with me, fully clothed or not. And as Markus had said, he didn't do unwilling women, which was a strangely comforting thought.

I grabbed the towel and the shirt and headed for the bathroom. I'd use the toilet and wash my face and consider taking a shower.

"Oh, wow." The bathroom was beautiful. Clean and all white, with straight lines and silver taps and fittings. There was a large walk-in shower and a double sink.

There was no way I could resist! I pushed the door shut and saw a nice large lock. "Yes." Decision made.

I slid the bolt into the slot and began to undress. I'd worked so many hours I was covered in dried sweat, grease and ketchup.

I shoved my skirt and ugly blouse combo to the floor and turned on the water. The shower was huge, made for at least two people. Maybe three.

My thoughts wandered to the brothers who would easily fit in here with a woman as well. *No. Don't go there.*

I tried not to think about how many women the guys had fucked in this shower. The men weren't mine. I had no right to be jealous, and yet my stomach tightened and lurched in a sickening swoop.

"Just don't think about it," I told myself as I stripped off my underwear, then scurried beneath the water. "Oh, wow."

The shower head was big and high pressure, something I had rarely experienced before.

I turned around and let the water beat down on my back. The door was locked, and I'd had one hell of a night. Surely, nothing else bad would happen to me?

As the thought resonated, I realized I should get into bed and have the police on speed dial, just in case. I was taking a huge risk here, and yet my instincts were telling me these guys were safe. That I could relax.

Not a feeling I'd had many times in my life, so I wasn't sure I could trust my gut instinct, even when it screamed at me that I was safe.

I scrubbed the stink of the day from my skin and switched off the water. When I reached for the towel, there was a soft knock on the door. "Lexi, it's just me, Ollie. I wanted to let you know there's fresh soap and shampoo under the sink. Help yourself."

I wrapped the towel around me as fast as I could, but he didn't attempt to open the door. "Thanks, Ollie, but I'm done."

"Okay, well. Good night!"

The sound of his footsteps disappearing down the hallway met my ears.

I would have cried if I was a crying type of girl. Had I seriously found a trustworthy man who wasn't going to try to force his way in here? *Two* trustworthy men?

I dried the rest of my body, hating the size of my thighs and the jiggling of my belly. I'd tried so many times to lose weight, but between stress eating and my hatred of exercise, I wasn't going to be a size eight anytime soon.

I folded up the towel and placed it on the edge of the double sink, then slid my arms into the large flannel shirt and buttoned up.

The scent of Ollie encased me. Warm and soft, much like the man himself.

I glanced in the mirror to make sure all my smudged mascara was washed off my face, grimacing at the unkept woman in the mirror. Then I shrugged. Not like I was on a date. I was going to sleep, and the guys would be in bed too, hopefully.

I picked up my pile of dirty clothes and unlocked the door before opening it a crack. There was no one in the hallway.

Pushing open the door, I went up on my tiptoes and crept down the hall to my room. My heart was thumping a little too fast, but I was worried about being caught.

I almost made it too. I was one step away from my door when Markus came bounding up the stairs. I rushed forward, but he stopped right in front of me, glaring hard. "What. Are. You. Wearing?"

I glanced down at the shirt that covered me to mid-thigh. I wasn't wearing any underwear and I was suddenly painfully aware of my naked pussy.

"Ah... Ollie gave me a shirt to wear to bed because I didn't have anything else."

I didn't know why I was defending myself, but Markus looked downright furious.

"Anyway..." What the hell was I supposed to say now? "Goodnight."

As I turned away, I noticed something off. Markus had his car keys in his hand. "Going somewhere?"

He glanced down at the keys, then back at me. "I was considering going back out... but I've changed my mind."

I tilted my head in confusion. "Going back out to St. Patrick's?"

The bar I was pretty sure he'd been at tonight. It was hot at the moment, always full of people.

Biggest pick-up place in the city.

He nodded.

I inhaled swiftly, a strange knife-like pain cutting into my diaphragm. I didn't like it. Markus's announcement. Or my reaction to it. "Oh... well, I'm sorry I mucked up your night. Please, go. I'm sure there're plenty of women there, anxious for you to bring them home. I can cook them breakfast in the morning. Waitress Lexie at your service."

I did a mock little curtsey, my temper getting the better of me again.

Markus was an insanely hot man. Standing there in a long sleeved white shirt and fitted blue jeans, he looked better than any billboard model I'd ever seen. He had huge arms and a wide chest tapering down to a flat stomach and smaller waist.

When my gaze finally lifted back to his eyes, the fury I'd seen moments before had been replaced by something more complicated. I couldn't read his expression at all.

I sighed, not sure what to say next. "Goodnight, Markus."

He advanced on me so fast I barely had time to drop my dirty clothes to the floor before he pushed me up against the doorframe, his huge body pinning me in place.

"I can get laid anytime I want, you know that? My phone's full of texts from women asking me to come out, come over. Every day of the week."

He wasn't making a move and he wasn't hurting me; he was just talking. And staring down at me like he wasn't sure what he wanted to do with me.

I slowly raised my hands, grateful for the layers of clothing between us.

Pressing my palms to his chest, I felt the racing heartbeat beneath my fingers and saw the rapid rise and fall of his chest. "Then go," I whispered up at him, staring into his eyes that were so dark brown they were almost midnight in color.

"I can't," he ground out. "Not while you're here and wearing my brother's damn clothes."

My breath caught in my throat and my mouth dried like the Sahara.

I licked my lips to wet them and watched his gaze drop to zero in on my mouth.

"Do you want me to go?" I asked, feeling him shift and press his groin harder against me. The move shared the erection that was so big he couldn't hide it if he tried.

A lick of arousal hit right between my clenched thighs.

"You know I don't want that," he said, his voice rough.

I didn't want to ask. I shouldn't ask. And yet... "What *do* you want, Markus?"

His jaw tightened before he said one word. "This."

CHAPTER 5

MARKUS

As I thrust forward, pressing my rapidly thickening cock against her soft belly, I knew I was doing the wrong thing. I should be walking away, taking my hormones and uncontrollable lust back to the club where women welcomed it.

Not to the woman I had in my arms.

Not to a woman who was wearing my brother's clothes over her freshly naked body.

But there was no running away. My wolf growled *mate* inside my head. And all I could think about was stamping my scent all over her.

I stared at her mouth for half a moment, trying to rein myself in, aiming for some sort of control. But she lifted her chin in an age-old invitation to take what I wanted, and I was lost.

I kissed her, and the mere touch of her soft lips beneath mine dragged a loud moan from me. I cupped her face and devoured her mouth, needing her more than my next breath.

When she grabbed hold of my shirt and dragged me closer, I slanted my mouth over hers and speared my tongue in to taste her. She was everything I'd been afraid to dream of. Soft, luscious, sensual. She felt like home.

I don't know what stopped me, but the effect was as if someone had doused me with a bucket of cold water.

What am I doing?

I'd declared that she would be safe in my home. That I didn't take unwilling women to my bed. And although Lexi's clinging hands and soft gasps of pleasure were definitely signs that she wanted me, I couldn't believe that was the case. She was vulnerable, almost naked, and in a strange place.

I didn't take advantage of women. Ever.

So, what the fuck am I doing?

I pulled away and managed to get an inch of space between us. "I'm sorry, Lexi. I shouldn't have done that." Then I forced myself to take a large step back and leaned against the other side of the door frame, still facing her.

Damn, she's beautiful.

Her eyes were shining. Her cheeks were rosy, and her lips were swollen from my kisses.

If I ever in my whole life wanted to fuck a woman, it was this one. Right now.

And I couldn't.

Lexie rolled off the doorframe and into her room. "Ah... so, I suppose I should..."

I nodded sharply once. "Yep. Night."

I didn't get one step before she called out, "Can I ask you why?"

"Why what?"

"Why shouldn't you have done that? Because I'm... me? Or?" She was fidgeting with the sleeves on the shirt now, and although she looked extremely nervous, I could tell she wanted a real answer to the question.

I frowned. She thought I was rejecting her?

"No, well, yes. Fuck..." I ran a hand through my hair. "What I meant was... You're a guest in our home. I promised you we'd keep our hands to ourselves. And the first time I see you... like that..." I gestured to her long, shapely legs. "I jump you like a teenager with no control. I'm sorry. I..."

I was ashamed of my actions. But I couldn't get the words out properly.

She crossed her arms over her chest and looked down. Shit. I'd offended her, somehow. I had a younger sister. I knew what women looked like when they were upset.

I put both hands out and clung to the doorframe, not entering the room, but hovering as close to her as I dared. "Lexi, look at me."

She forced her head up and stared at me, her eyes no longer shining.

"Don't you dare think that I don't want you. Look at me. Isn't it obvious I do?"

Her gaze flicked down to my erection that was impossible to hide, then back up to my face. She pressed her lips into a thin line. What the hell? Had I just pissed her off again?

I groaned, confused. "What did I say?"

"Nothing." She shook her head. "I just... wanna go to bed, okay?"

"Sure. Good night."

She walked forward and practically shut the door in my face.

The sound of the lock clicking into place made me clench my jaw. If I didn't take advantage of her when she wanted me to, I certainly wasn't going to force myself on her any other time.

I stomped to my room and slammed the door shut behind me.

Dammit.... Fucking... Grr...

I allowed my wolf to surface so a real growl rolled up through my vocal cords. I couldn't seem to say anything right.

How could she be my mate if we clashed at every meeting?

My mate. Fucking hell! This was the last thing I expected. I didn't want a mate. Never had.

I paced the floor in front of my bed, over and over.

I was sure Ollie could hear me.

In fact, I was pretty sure Ollie had heard the entire conversation between us, and he hadn't come out.

I stopped pacing. That rat. He wanted us to get together because Ollie knew that once I touched my mate, I wouldn't want to stop touching her.

"Motherfucker!"

I dropped to the ground and started doing push-ups. *One. Two.*

How was I going to get out of this mess?

Three. Four.

My cock was aching, my body on fire. I wanted her so badly.

Five. Six.

My phone dinged and I rolled into a sitting position to look down at the screen. It was past two a.m. now.

The message was from Nancy, another wolf shifter. Her sex drive was insanely high, and we often used each other for a workout when the need struck.

Had done for years.

Hey. You alone? Up for some company?

I tapped on the screen to reply and froze. Was I up for some company? Hell, yes!

Hers? Ah… no. All I could think about was Lexie just down the hall.

I turned off my phone and ignored her text.

She knew I was busy if I didn't respond. Better she thought I was with someone else than actively rejecting her. Not that Nancy was particularly thin-skinned, but her ego would thank me.

More push-ups built up a sweat but didn't do anything for the sexual frustration beating through me like a caveman with a club.

What was wrong with me?

Lexie wasn't even my type! She was too… I don't know. Too sweet, maybe? And yet, there was a hidden fire within her that I fucking loved.

I dropped to the floor and whacked my forehead against the carpet. "Fuck."

She was sexy, definitely. Even though I'd never been with a woman as curvy as her, my hands ached to grip her ass and feel the heavy flesh in my hands. And those breasts... damn, I could get lost in them.

Jumping to my feet, I stripped off my shirt. There was only one thing that was going to settle me down.

I headed for the shower, where I stood beneath the same hot spray Lexie had been under only an hour before.

There, I let my imagination go wild. Lexie in front of me, bent over and waiting for me to slide my cock into her.

Lexie on her knees, sucking me.

Lexie on her back, her huge breasts soft and her nipples hard. I would suck on those pink tips until she cried out to me...

I pumped my hand hard along my shaft until I blew, coming all over the shower tiles.

My loud groan filled the space and I closed my eyes, enjoying the pulses of heated pleasure coursing over my body and draining away at least some of the frustration and need.

I cleaned up quickly, turned off the water and dried myself. It was definitely time for bed, and now that I'd fixed myself up, hopefully sleep would come quickly.

I wrapped the towel around my waist and swayed where I stood, lethargy stealing through my muscles and relaxing me in a way that only an orgasm could.

My bedroom was only a few feet away from the bathroom door, but I still made sure my towel was tightly fastened before walking out into the hallway and making my way to my room.

The last thing I wanted was to run into Lexie like this. She probably thought I was some sort of lecherous asshole, hitting on her when she was barely dressed.

I growled as I shut the door, threw the towel over the hook, and crawled into my cold bed.

Not the way I'd hoped to be spending my Saturday night.

I'd thought by now I'd be balls deep in a warm woman, not lying here grappling with the idea that I may have found my mate. The very concept sounded wrong to my ears.

I lifted my arm and lay it across my face, covering my eyes with my forearm.

"Damn it all to hell."

A perfect Fated mate was Ollie's dream, not mine. And just because we were a perfect pair, didn't mean we had to share a mate.

It wasn't fair. It wasn't how I wanted to spend my life. And surely, Fate understood that?

If I stayed away or even moved out, maybe Ollie and Lexie could just get together and leave me out of it.

The very idea of my brother mating with the woman I wanted turned my insides upside down, but better to deal with some short-term stress, rather than long-term agony.

I wasn't built for monogamy and fidelity and proved it time and time again.

My sister told me I wasn't.

Every woman I'd ever dated told me the same thing.

Surely, I didn't need another woman to tell me what I already knew? I wasn't built to be a husband. Especially not to a woman as beautiful and special as Lexie. She deserved someone who could be completely faithful and monogamous. Someone who would worship her, body and soul. I couldn't give her that.

It would be best for both of us if I just left her alone.

CHAPTER 6

LEXIE

A soft knock on my door roused me from one of the best sleeps of my life. "Come in," I managed to mumble, though I wasn't sure yet who I was talking to.

Why was someone knocking...Was it a nurse? Was I in hospital? That would make sense as to why I had been so deeply asleep.

I forced my eyes to open, though they felt weighed down as if by lead.

There was a man standing quietly beside my bed, sporting a soft smile and holding a tray of food. Ollie.

My brain finally woke up properly. That's right. I was at Markus and Oliver's house.

I pushed down the covers that I had pulled up to my chin and glanced around.

"Good morning," I managed and dragged myself up to a sitting position. "I'm so sorry if I slept in."

Ollie chuckled good naturedly. "Don't ever apologize for getting the rest you obviously need. I should apologize for waking you, but your brunch was getting cold, and I was... honestly, wanting to see you. Slide back."

I moved as he requested, rearranging the pillows so I could sit with my back against the headboard, and luckily remembered to push the shirt down to cover my bare belly and lower.

"Here you go," he said, sliding the tray onto my lap. "I wasn't sure what you liked, or if you had any food allergies, or were a vegan, so I kinda covered all the bases just in case."

Staring down at the laden tray, I couldn't help but laugh at his warmhearted nature and intent. "Well, I've worked hospitality for five years, so I understand the worry. But no allergies here, luckily, and full meat eater."

Not that I often had enough money to eat as well as I wished. Eating cheap often meant eating crappy food.

"This is just... wow. Thank you." The tray was covered with our entire breakfast menu at the diner, all arranged on little plates. Eggs and bacon, toast and butter, sliced up fruit and a container of yogurt.

"You're welcome," Ollie said, grabbing the chair that looked matched the desk in the room, and sitting down beside the bed. "Please eat."

I picked up the bacon and placed it on the toast, choosing to start with a sandwich of sorts. "Have you had breakfast?"

He grinned. "Yeah, hours ago."

"Hours ago?" I repeated. "What time is it?"

"Nearly one o'clock."

I almost choked on my toast, but managed to chew it enough to force it down before I asked, "In the afternoon?"

Ollie chuckled. "Well, you didn't go to bed until, what? One-thirty?"

"Yeah... but I never sleep this late." I couldn't believe it. I'd never slept in until the afternoon. Ever.

But then again, I hadn't plugged my phone in for my alarm to go off, so it was probably dead in my bag.

Ollie shrugged like it was no big deal. "You obviously needed it."

I sighed and reached for a slice of banana. "Thank you so much for this, Ollie. For breakfast and for being so patient with me today.

You probably had plans and need to go out. I'll pack up as soon as I can."

Ollie held up both hands. "Oh, no, that wasn't the reason I woke you up. I don't have anything I need to be doing. Well, I plan to go with you to wherever you've been staying and get all your stuff. You can stay here as long as you want. This bedroom is almost always free."

I noticed he didn't say that I could leave when I wanted. I wasn't sure I'd ever actually *want* to leave a place I felt so safe.

"Ah... I don't know what to say." I wasn't used to people being generous with me.

"Say you'll stay for a while," Ollie said with a grin on his gorgeous face. His eyes were as blue as the sky and his hair was a lot blonder in the daylight than I had realized last night.

Markus was the dark one. Dark hair. Dark eyes. Dark mood.

Ollie was full of lightness.

"I'll look for another job first thing tomorrow," I said, pulling myself away from musing about the brothers' good looks and focusing on a plan for my future.

He shrugged. "Whatever. We're not strapped for cash. We don't expect you to pay for anything, so no hurry."

"What do you do?" I asked, taking another bite of the crispy, greasy bacon. My stomach was in heaven.

"I'm an accountant," he said, as though that wasn't a big deal.

It was for me! "Wow." College educated. White collar.

He wasn't what I expected an accountant to look like. Weren't they all nerdy?

He shrugged. "And Markus does garden landscaping. Private contracts, stuff like that."

I smiled at him. "The brains and the brawn, huh?"

He blinked at me as though I shouldn't have said such a thing. I probably shouldn't.

"Not that I was inferring you don't have brawn! Or that Markus doesn't have a brain," I reassured him, reaching for his arm. "You're gorgeous! I didn't mean to offend, I promise. It was a silly thing to say."

Instead of yelling at me or stomping off like I half expected, Ollie laughed. "Oh, no. That's not it. It wasn't silly. Markus does have a lot more muscle than me. About fifty pounds worth. I just found it interesting that you instantly saw the way we complement each other."

I tilted my head at him, my intuition picking up on something strange in his tone. This conversation was important to him and for some reason, he thought it may be important to me also.

I never ignored my intuition. "You know," I said, "I was really worried about coming back here last night. I thought I'd never be able to fall sleep because I'd be too scared. And yet I slept, the best I have in... well, forever."

Ollie's eyes lit up with obvious happiness. "That's great. I hope you always feel safe and secure here."

"Can I ask you something?" I questioned, taking a spoon full of the rich yogurt, loving the assortment of flavors and textures that he'd added into my breakfast—or rather, given the time of day, my lunch.

He nodded. "Anything."

"What's with your brother?"

Ollie burst out laughing. "Ah... that is too broad a question to even begin to answer. Can you be more specific?"

"Well, I mean... you're so different, and yet you're also similar. You're both good men, obviously, trustworthy and caring. You proved that last night. But Markus seems, totally different from you. I don't know. I probably sound ridiculous."

I wasn't sure what I was asking, and realized I wasn't being specific at all. I decided I needed to focus on my food rather than unravel this mystery right now. I took a sip from the glass of orange juice on the corner of the tray and took a bite of a sliced apple.

Ollie put his hand out and pressed against my knee. "Actually, you don't sound ridiculous at all. Thing is, Markus and I aren't just brothers, we're twins."

"Twins?" I asked, shocked. "Fraternal, obviously."

"Yeah. Obviously. But we're, um…" He shook his head suddenly. "I wasn't sure if I should tell you this yet or not."

"Tell me," I said, feeling my intuition kick in again regarding the inevitability of this conversation.

He sighed. "Well, in our pa… err… family, there's something called a perfect pair. It pretty much means a fraternal set of twins that are the opposite from each other in every way. One light, one dark. One tall and big, one shorter and smaller. One brains, one brawn. Usually, Markus is more light-hearted and funnier than me. I'm more serious. It's like the list of every quality available got evenly divided up and distributed between us."

My brows rose as he spoke. Sounded like perfection all tied up in two men rather than one. "But you're both kind and generous," I said. "And you have manners. It's not like one of you is all nice and the other one is a serial killer, or something."

Well, I hoped not, anyway.

Ollie cackled at that. "Ah, yeah. Well, our Mom would kick our asses if we didn't show a basic level of respect. Especially toward women."

I liked that. She sounded like my sort of woman. A mother someone could actually look up to. One I wished I'd had.

"And your dad?" I asked, trying not to sound too nosy, yet I wanted to know everything about these incredible men.

"What about him?"

"Is he… still around? Or did your mom raise you on her own?" I wouldn't have been surprised, of course. Half of modern marriages ended in divorce.

"Oh, he's very much still around," Ollie said. "He's a good man. You'd like him, I think."

Something strange and warm curled around my heart that I couldn't describe, but it was simultaneously uncomfortable and a feeling I wanted to experience again.

"I'm sure I would," I managed before pushing the tray off my lap. "I need to run to the bathroom, sorry."

"Cool," Ollie said, hopping to his feet and racing ahead of me to the door. "I'll go get ready, and we can fetch your things."

"Yeah. Thanks."

Ollie left and I hopped out of bed, tugging the shirt down as far as possible, then racing for the bathroom.

I couldn't hear any other noises in the house, so I had to assume that Markus had gone out for the day.

Probably off chasing one of the many women he was talking about last night.

When I got back to my room, I slid on the fresh clothes from my bag. I was a little cold, but at least I'd packed fresh underwear.

When I grabbed my bag and walked out into the hall, I heard Ollie call out, "Hey, Lexie! Wanna swing by the diner and see if we can get your pay as well?"

Damn, I would love that! But... "Not sure my boss will be in today." He probably would be, but the last thing I wanted to do was confront him.

Made me sick to my stomach to think about dealing with him, especially after the scene I'd caused last night.

I trotted down the stairs and shivered at the cool breeze coming in the open front door. "Damn... didn't pack a sweater."

Ollie immediately turned and picked up a hoodie that was sitting folded on the back of the couch. "I thought you might need one. Not sure it'll fit, but at least you'll be warm."

It fit better than it should have. It was big in the shoulders, but too tight around my hips.

I tugged at it self-consciously. "I hope I don't stretch it for you. My ass is too big, and my hips are rather wide. I'm sorry."

Ollie snorted. "You're fucking perfect. Don't worry about any such nonsense."

It was the first time I'd heard him swear, and although it almost sounded odd coming from him, the rest of his words certainly had the impact he'd aimed for.

I was stunned. "Ah..."

"Let's go," he said, swinging his car keys around his finger in a loop. "We can go get your stuff, then chill for a while. Take-out for dinner, maybe?"

I nodded in agreement as we walked out the front door and toward his truck. I felt as comfortable in his presence as if we'd been dating for years instead of having known each other less than twenty-four hours.

I wasn't sure what to make of the easy camaraderie, and I wasn't ready to ask him, in case that popped the illusion like a bubble.

I hopped in the car, toasty warm thanks to the hooded sweatshirt I wore that smelled of Ollie.

"So, where to?" he asked, turning on the engine.

"Oh, yes. An apartment on Castle Road."

"Great."

Ollie drove and I directed, and fifteen minutes later we were standing outside the rundown restaurant that I called home. Or had, for the last twelve months.

"I..." I swallowed hard. "I'm not one hundred percent sure he's going to let me in."

"Because of the owed rent?" Ollie asked, seeming a little nonplussed.

I nodded, my stomach twisting. I hated admitting that I was behind and failing at such a basic life skill as paying my own bills. Ollie was successful. He had a good job. A house. He probably wouldn't understand what it was like to have nothing.

My cheeks heated with shame, but Ollie didn't seem judgmental in any way. He just turned to me and said, "Well, let's go see, shall we?"

He took my hand and little frissons of electricity skittled across my skin.

I gripped his hand harder, as if I could keep a man like him on his feet. "You're not gonna keel over again, are you?"

He laughed, then tugged my hand and together we ran across the road. "No. I think I'm pretty good right now."

"What was that all about?" I asked, realizing I'd never asked. "The whole, weird, falling down thing you and your brother did."

Ollie wasn't looking at me now. "It's a family trait. I'll explain it to you another time. Let's get this sorted for you first."

I nodded and pulled my keys out of my bag. "There's an external entrance up those stairs."

I headed toward the fire escape only to find a note pinned to the ladder. *Lexie. Come in through the front.*

My heart lurched. "Uh-oh." That wasn't a good sign. I wasn't sure what he was expecting, but I had nothing to offer the old man who'd rented the apartment to me. Nothing but more empty promises and the truth about my pay, which he was going to see as an excuse.

Ollie smiled gently, full of confidence. "Don't stress. We can sort this out. It's only money."

I almost rolled my eyes. Only people who had enough money said, "It's only money." I'd never known that feeling.

Ollie walked me around to the front of the restaurant and pushed open the door, the bells ringing above our heads.

"Lexie, girl. Where's my money?"

I suppressed the shiver of fear that coursed down my back. "Hello, Mr. Lee. I'm very sorry, but my boss hasn't paid me for the last two weeks, and he fired me last night."

The old Chinese man scrunched up his face. "No rent, no access to room. I will have to try and sell whatever you have up there."

"Oh, please, no. Don't do that. I'll figure something out."

My cheeks were blazing. If it wasn't bad enough that I had to beg to get access to my clothes, Ollie was here to witness it as well.

Ollie put a hand on my shoulder. "Lexie, go up and grab whatever you need. I'm sure the gentleman and I can come to an agreement."

Mr. Lee stared at Ollie for a moment, then nodded once.

"Ollie. No... I..."

"Go. It's all good," he said, as cool and calm as any man I'd ever seen.

"Ah... okay." I raced out of the restaurant and up the fire escape, which was the only entrance to my apartment.

It was only one room, a studio with a tiny bathroom and toilet next to the even smaller kitchen space. But it had been safe and relatively clean.

And it had been mine.

I grabbed my old black suitcase and duffle bag and began to pack, prioritizing things I couldn't replace. Photos. Identifying documents. Some hidden emergency cash that was nowhere near enough for rent.

More like a dinner or two.

Then clothes. The warmest, best fitting.

When my two bags were packed, I glanced around at everything I was leaving behind. Some blankets and pillows. Clothes and books. But I couldn't carry them, and I wasn't asking Ollie to come up here with me.

I walked out onto the fire escape and Ollie called up to me, "Toss anything down you want me to carry."

I threw him the duffle bag first, then the suitcase.

"Anything else?"

I shook my head and carefully—because I was very likely to slip on the ladder and fall on Ollie's head—climbed down once more.

"Everything okay with Mr. Lee?" I asked, trying to hide the fact I was puffing a little from the descent.

"Yep."

Ollie turned and began walking back toward the truck.

I followed him, a little relieved but confused. "What happened in there? Did you get an extension for me?"

"Yeah, kind of." Ollie opened the truck and slid my bag and the suitcase behind the seats. "I paid your rent, so you're a month in advance now. You can move back, or just use it as a place to chill out or study. Or whatever else you might need."

He was still loading my stuff in, but I was really confused now. "Hang on a minute. You paid my rent? For last month and this month?"

I didn't believe him. That was almost two thousand dollars. Why would he do that for someone he didn't even know?

"Yeah. So, if you didn't get everything, you can always come back tomorrow or whenever. Hop in."

I did as he asked, getting in the truck because I wanted to go back to his nice, clean house and have take-out for dinner, but I still had no idea why he'd done what he'd done.

The only reason someone had helped me in the past was because they wanted something from me. Sex or something equally gross, usually.

I didn't want to insult him by insinuating that he'd been kind so he could get something out of me, though I didn't have any other answer.

"Ollie, sorry to ask, again. I'm so incredibly grateful, but... why did you just pay all that money for me?"

He shrugged as he turned on the truck's engine. "You needed help. I'm happy to give it."

I could feel the truth behind his words, but there was so much more to it. "Ollie, what am I to you? A charity case?"

He laughed and my brows came together. I felt like getting out of the car and walking.

"No. No, I'm sorry," he said, grabbing my arm before I reached for the car door. "Listen, you are not a charity case."

"Then what am I?"

He sighed, then said in a voice I'd never forget as long as I lived. "Sweetheart, you're my whole heart. You're my future. You're my everything."

CHAPTER 7

OLIVER

I could see from Lexie's shocked expression that I'd gone too far, and immediately wanted to take every word back. I meant them, of course, but it was too soon for her to hear them, or understand about our fated connection.

I turned off the ignition and tried not to let my impatience shine through. I wanted my mate where she belonged. In my arms. In my bed. In my heart.

"It's okay," I said, glad my voice was steady. "If you want to get out, I'll help you with your bags. But I'd much rather you stay in the truck, and let me take you back to our place."

I risked a glance at her and saw the indecision on her features. Her eyebrows were twisted and she was chewing on her bottom lip, an action that just made my heart pound a little faster.

Damn, she was beautiful. I'd never get used to looking at her gorgeous mouth, her delectable curves and her bright, intelligent eyes.

She twisted in her seat to face me. "I don't... can you explain what you mean by that?"

I nodded, tamping down the sick feeling in my stomach. Had I pushed too fast, too soon? "I can. Here or at home?"

She chewed some more on her bottom lip. I barely stopped myself from leaning over and kissing her. I had to grip the steering wheel hard, then turn and stare out the windshield.

"No, I suppose we can go back to your place and chat," she said at last. "It's a lot nicer than my place."

I chuckled. Although what she said was true, I didn't think that admitting I'd live with her anywhere—even in a tree if it came to that—would go down well at this point in time.

"No problem. Do you want to go past the diner and pick anything up?"

She nodded. "Actually, yes, please."

I drove her the ten minutes back to the establishment where I'd first run into her. She hopped out of the truck and called in through the window, "I'll only be one minute. Left my phone charger inside."

She didn't give me time to agree, she just ran inside. I put the truck into park and watched her through the window.

It was hard to believe that only last night I'd been lamenting the fact that I hadn't met my mate yet. That I wanted her more than anything. Then Fate had served Lexie up to me, making me literally crash into her.

It was said that the electrical touch that mates shared was the way Fate made sure you didn't miss each other. That it was an obvious sign that made you sit up and take notice.

Well, I was listening and had taken notice. I was wide awake and willing to do anything necessary to keep Lexie in my life.

Markus, on the other hand... I wasn't sure what that idiot was going to do. He was as connected to Lexie as I was. She was made for us, as we were made for her. Our perfect mate, and for her, we would be the perfect pair.

But that didn't mean Markus would automatically do what was in his best interest. I'd seen him blow off awesome business opportunities and even great girlfriends in the past, all because of the delusional idea that he didn't deserve such things.

Lexie came running out of the diner, her face a hot, red mess. "What happened?" I asked, reaching over to touch her arm.

"Nothing. Can we please just go?"

A big man with a red nose came barreling out of the diner. "Don't you ever come back, you hear me? Damn trailer trash. I should never have given you a job in the first place."

Lexie's eyes filled with tears at the same rate anger filled my gut.

I reached for the door handle, ready to jump from the truck to tell this guy where to go, but Lexie reached for me, holding tightly to my arm. "No. Please. Let's just go."

"He needs some sense beaten into him," I growled, glaring at the guy hard enough that he had the good sense to take a step back.

"No. Please," she sobbed.

I couldn't fight him now. Lexie would burst into tears, and I couldn't have that. So, I put the vehicle into gear and took off.

Fighting that asshole was going to make her more upset, and it wasn't like she needed the money. I'd pay for everything, for as long as she wanted. I'd worked hard to pay off my half of our house, and despite his resistance, so had Markus.

We were ready for the next stage of our life, in most senses of the word.

"What did he say to upset you so much?" I asked Lexie as she frantically wiped at the tears on her face.

"Oh, not much more than you already heard," she said. "He said I was a loser. A waste of space. A fat... lard."

An inhuman growl vibrated through my vocal cords as Lexie stopped speaking to sob once more.

I forced my wolf down and spoke softly, "Listen to me, sweetheart. You are the most beautiful woman I have ever seen, and I don't want you worried about money or a new job. Or any of that shit. Okay? It isn't important."

She didn't answer me, instead mopping her face and blowing her nose. She wouldn't be able to understand what I was offering her at this time. Not yet. Not until we explained the Fated mate bond, and even then, I wasn't sure how she was going to feel about the ménage à trois component. Until then, all I could do was try and make her feel better.

"Let's go to the store, and we'll buy chocolate and ice cream and whatever candy you want, then go home and watch a movie. How 'bout that?"

She wiped at another tear that slid down her cheek. "Why are you being so nice to me?"

I pulled the truck into the closest supermarket and turned off the ignition. "Think of it as fate that I found you, and you found me. Now... tell me about you."

"What do you want to know?" she asked, her shoulders slouched and defeated-looking.

"Well, how old are you? Where are you from? Anything you want to tell me." When she didn't start talking, I gave it a go. "Okay, I'll start. I'm thirty. An accountant for the largest firm in the city. Love numbers. Don't love my job, but it pays the bills. I'm super close with my family but can be a bit of a loner. Don't go out much. Um... and I haven't traveled much yet but would love to start."

She gave me half a smile. "I'm twenty-six. Barely finished high school, never went to college. I grew up in the south. Poor. Very poor. Got out when I turned eighteen and I've been living hand to mouth ever since."

"Let's go." I tilted my head toward the store, then got out of the truck.

She came with me and when she closed her door, I walked around and reached for her hand, walking inside the market with a skip in my step. "Then you've achieved more than I have in my whole life, Lexie. I had it easy. Good family. Support. College scholarship. I don't know anyone who would have survived the start you got, myself included. You're amazing."

She gave me a proper smile this time and moved closer to my side.

I felt like a king as we walked into the store, Lexie on my arm, wearing my hoodie. I wanted to tell the world that she was mine, and I'd start with the first person I saw.

We made our way to the candy aisle and loaded up on everything I thought we'd like.

She only chose one bar and I laughed. "You're kidding, right? Go nuts. Get everything and anything."

I respected the fact that she obviously wasn't a "taker," but I wanted her to be happy. "Markus loves anything with chocolate and nuts, so grab some stuff for him too."

She perked up at that idea, starting to choose more bags and bars of chocolate.

We loaded everything into a basket and set off for the registers.

"Hey! Ollie," a woman's voice called out and I cringed. I knew that voice. Of all the people to run into...

"Please play along with whatever I say," I whispered to Lexie. At her small nod, I turned around. "Nancy. Hey."

I put my arm around Lexie's shoulders and pulled her tightly into my side.

Nancy, who was a rather stunning female wolf shifter we'd grown up with, sauntered up to us with a come-hither smile on her face.

"Who have you got there?" Nancy asked, giving Lexie an assessing look that would have made most women wither up and die.

Lexie cringed but didn't step away. Instead, she curled into me a little more.

I stood straighter, raising my chin. "This is Lexie, my mate."

Nancy's jaw dropped and I would have high-fived Lexie if she'd known how much of a win that was. "Your *what*? Since when?"

"Since yesterday," I said with a smile. "We were on our way home, so should I give Markus a message for you, or..."

Nancy narrowed her eyes. "Yeah, just tell him to call me." There was an edge in her tone, and she shot another look at Lexie that held no warmth whatsoever.

I put my body squarely between the two women, my protective instinct toward Lexie rising. "No problem," I said, gently pushing Lexie toward the registers. "Here, honey." I gave her my credit card in front of Nancy, much to Lexie's obvious surprise.

But to her credit, she looked at Nancy and said, "Nice to meet you." Then she went through the register to collect our candy and tap my card.

I nodded at the female wolf shifter, my narrowed eyes daring her to step forward and interact with my mate in any way that wasn't respectful. If she did, there'd be consequences.

Nancy must have sensed it, because her body relaxed into a slightly more submissive posture and she dropped her voice to a whisper. "She's human."

I shrugged. "So?"

"And she's... what about Markus?"

I shrugged again. "My brother will make up his own mind."

Her eyes lit up at the prospect of still claiming Markus as her own. What she didn't realize was that my brother had never thought of Nancy as more than a friend with benefits.

She'd never be his mate, and that should be obvious to her now.

I waved at her and walked through the registers to Lexie, whose eyes were flashing with anger. "Who. Was. That?"

"A family friend," I said, taking the plastic bags from her. "And to answer the question I can see burning in your eyes—have I slept with her? Absolutely not."

Her shoulders relaxed slightly at my words, and she walked with me to the truck before suddenly asking, "What about Markus?"

I opened the door and put the bags inside. "You'll have to speak to my brother about that. His past is... how should I say it? More colorful than mine, but it's his right to speak about that, not mine."

"You've never been married?" she asked as we slid into the seats.

I laughed. "Not even close."

"No serious girlfriends?"

I smiled. "Nope. I was waiting for the one."

She didn't ask any more questions, but I could almost hear all the thoughts burning in her brain the whole way home.

CHAPTER 8
MARKUS

I'd left home around nine in the morning, hoping not to encounter either my brother or Lexie. It had been a sin to get up that early on a Sunday morning, but neither my wolf nor I could sleep any longer. Ollie had been in the shower, and I couldn't hear Lex moving about. So as soon as I was up and dressed, I headed for the gym, then to the nearby diner for lunch.

After that, I hadn't known what to do, so I'd gone over to a buddy's place for a beer and a game of pool, delaying going home as long as I could. The worst part about it was the fact that it wasn't like I didn't *want* to go home. If anything, it fucking hurt to stay away, which made me work even harder not to fall into the trap Lexie and Fate were setting for me.

I shouldn't be aching for a woman I'd barely kissed, surely? I couldn't be jealous that my brother was spending the day with a woman he believed was his mate. *Our* mate. Could I?

Of course, not. So, whatever this horrible, twisted, sickening feeling was in my gut, it could fuck right off.

By six o'clock, I was freaking dying. I couldn't stay away any longer.

I headed home, half hoping Lexie would be gone, and half praying she'd be lying on the couch ready with a welcoming smile for me. My feelings were all churned up inside. I had no idea what I wanted, or what I'd be walking into, but it was time to find out.

When I parked my truck in the driveway behind Ollie's vehicle, my heart rate picked up.

I sat there in the driver's seat as long as I could, trying to work out what I actually wanted. Did I want to walk inside and see my brother happily cuddled up with his mate? How would that make me feel? Would I be pleased for him? Or jealous as fuck?

My fingers tightened on the wheel as my phone buzzed from beside me. I'd been ignoring the damn thing most of the day, but when I glanced over at the screen, I saw Ollie's familiar text bubble.

You comin' inside? We're looking at dinner options. You wanna weigh in?

He said "we". *Fuck.*

I slid out of the truck and slow-jogged up to the front door, a strangely excited buzz coursing through me. A feeling I'd never known before. Half happiness, half... I wasn't sure. But it wasn't fear, it was something else. Something primal. A feeling that I generally only got when I was in wolf form.

I tried to shake off the strange sensation and stay calm and focused. Unfortunately, I didn't have much success with that.

I opened the front door of my home and the first thing I smelled was Lexie's delicious perfume. It was a subtle flower aroma mixed with her own individual skin scent. I fucking loved it. One whiff, and my dick was already on its way to being hard.

I shut the door, stifling a groan, and hung up my keys on one of the hooks before heading into the main living room.

That's when I froze.

My heart hurt.

There, on our massive sectional couch, was Lexie curled up with Ollie. She had her head on his lap and his hand was tangled in her hair.

The coffee table was littered with bowls of candy and popcorn, cans of soda and a single beer.

I was hit with the strangest feeling, like I was viewing a snapshot in time.

My future. Right there, in front of me. *If* I wanted it.

I gulped down the sudden fear that rose inside my chest, prickly and hot.

I *couldn't* want it. It didn't suit me or my chosen lifestyle. This future wasn't for the likes of me.

"Hey," I managed, somehow, despite the churning in my gut.

Lexie sat up and rearranged her legs until she was sitting like a genie on the couch next to Ollie. "Hey."

My heart was pounding. She was so kissable, her pillowy, red lips calling to me.

My fingers tightened into fists as I tried to control my inner urge to leap across the room and take her in my arms. I crossed my arms over my chest, so I didn't follow my instincts. Damn, I wanted to hold her. So bad.

Ollie studied me for a moment before picking up the remote and pausing the movie they'd been watching. I hadn't even noticed the TV was on. "We were gonna order some pizza. You want your regular order, Markus, or you want Mexican or something?"

I looked from my brother to the woman sitting next to him, then back again. "Um... pizza. Fine. Yep."

I sounded like a caveman, but my brain felt fuzzy. I didn't know what I could do to utter more than monosyllabic grunts. That was all that was coming out right now.

Lexie turned to Ollie. "Can we chat now that Markus is back?"

Ollie chuckled, smiling at her with more love and warmth than I'd ever seen on my brother's face before.

Jealousy flared, and I bit out in a more caustic tone than I intended, "Whatcha talking about?"

Ollie looked at me, his gaze cooling. "We ran into Nancy at the grocery store, and Lexie has some questions about us... and our intentions, and a few other things."

I groaned and rolled my eyes. Of course, they'd walked into Nancy. Of all the fucking women... "I... can I have a shower first?"

Surely, they'd give me a minute to get my head on straight.

Lexie's lips twisted, then she nodded. "Okay. But you're coming back. Right?"

The fact that she wanted me here for this conversation as well as Ollie, and seemed anxious that I may leave again, made a strange feeling pass through my chest.

I couldn't identify it, but I wasn't leaving if she wanted me to stay. It would take a direct order from the pack Alpha to move me, and even then, I had the feeling I'd put up a fight.

"Sure. Be back in ten."

"Cool," Ollie said, reaching for his cell. "I'll order the pizzas."

Lexie smiled at me, her eyes shining in a way that once again, made me want to stay.

"I'll, ah..." I pointed to upstairs, and she nodded.

"See you soon, Markus."

I forced myself to turn and bolt up the stairs, half afraid that if I stayed, I wouldn't take the time I needed to breathe.

See you soon, Markus. Her voice when she said it had been laced with warmth. Matching heat seemed to infuse my limbs as I undressed and turned on the water. I couldn't get the effect of her presence out of my system. And to be honest, I wasn't certain I wanted to.

The shower washed away the stress and sweat of the day. I'd really pushed myself at the gym and could smell the effects of it. I lathered up extra hard, wanting to be clean and fresh when I headed downstairs again.

By the time I was dry and dressed, I heard the doorbell peel. A sign the pizzas were likely here.

What was I going to say to Lexie? What had my brother already told her?

Honesty was always the best policy, but were we going to reveal the shifter element, or not? That information wasn't shared with humans unless absolutely necessary, and we barely knew her.

"Thanks, bud," Ollie was saying at the door as I jogged down the stairs. He grabbed the pizzas from whoever was outside and shut the front door.

I met him in the lounge, where he was handing Lexie a pizza box.

"Here." Ollie handed me mine, and I sat down to devour the family-sized meatasaurus feast.

Ollie had his regular order, a supreme with extra cheese, but I was interested in what Lexie had. Was she one of those girls that would order a vegetarian to save calories, then barely eat a bite?

She opened her box to reveal a pizza loaded up with ingredients, and a cheesy smell wafted my way. "Oh, this smells amazing," she said. "Thank you, Ollie."

My brother grinned at her, and she got to eating.

I glanced over at the half empty bowls of snacks and had to assume she'd eaten some of those too. Despite myself, I was impressed. She could eat.

Thank God.

"So what else did you guys get up to today?" I asked. "Other than candy shopping..." *And running into my occasional booty call.*

Ollie opened a can of soda, the crack, pop and hiss sounding loud in the room. "We went over to Lexie's apartment, sorted out her rent and got some clothes."

"But you're still staying here, right?" I'd asked the question before I was able to moderate my tone. I sounded half desperate.

Lexie grabbed a napkin to wipe pizza sauce off her chin. "For the moment, yeah. Ollie offered, and, well... I'd rather stay here until I can get another job and pay you guys back for everything you've done already."

"Pay us back for what?" I asked.

Ollie glared at me. Oh. He'd *sorted out* her rent issue.

Then I looked at Lexie, and her face was glowing red with embarrassment. *Shit!* "Doesn't that asshole diner owner owe you a stack of money?"

She nodded. "Yeah, I went by to get my charger today, but he... Well..."

I narrowed my eyes at her look of shame, then switched to Ollie. "What did he do?"

"Ran her off, basically."

"How much does he owe you?" I asked.

She shrugged. "I don't know exactly. Two weeks' pay, plus he's held onto all the tips I've made since I started. He said he'd give them to me eventually, but..." She shrugged.

"He hasn't given you any of your tips? For the whole time?"

At her head shake, I only just suppressed a growl. "Figure it out for me," I told her. "I'll sort it out."

I fucking hated bullies. Especially men who preyed on women.

"Oh, no, please don't. I'll just get another job and go from there."

I smiled at her, working hard to soften my tone. "Could you please figure it out for me? I've got some friends in the industry. I might be able to sort something out for you."

"A new job?"

I shrugged. "Sure." But if Ollie had his way, she'd never work again. He'd always wanted a woman to spoil, to love, to...

Lexie sat up straighter, flicking her long, dark hair over her shoulder and rapidly changed the subject. "So, can you tell me more about the twin thing? And the mate thing, and everything?" She stared between us, waiting expectantly.

I reached for a beer that was sitting on the coffee table. I was gonna need one.

"Well, yeah. Sure," Ollie said, putting his half-eaten pizza down on the couch next to him. "How much do you know about wolf shifters?"

Lexie's eyebrows lifted high on her forehead. "Ah... *what*? Sorry, I think I misheard."

She glanced over at me, confusion clouding her eyes. I glared at

Ollie, who said to me, "Everything we have to tell her is based on the paranormal element. It won't make sense otherwise."

"But you know the rules."

Ollie sighed and turned to Lexie. "What we're about to tell you is a pretty tightly held secret, and although I'm totally comfortable telling you, because I want you as part of our life... If it doesn't work out, you can't tell anyone."

Lexie huffed out a soft laugh. "I grew up in a biker gang. I've seen more things and held more secrets than most. You don't need to worry about me."

A ton of questions immediately popped into my mind. What gang? Why? How? Was she okay? But I put the beer to my lips and swallowed the questions down for another time.

"Okay, well, basically Markus and I were born wolf shifters. We're part of a large pack in town that is integrated into the human world here. We're not werewolves, and we don't lose control of ourselves or turn into monsters at the full moon. We simply can turn into wolves and back again whenever we want."

There was a lot more to it, of course. Our hierarchy, our strength and speed. Not to mention the fact that the perfect pair phenomena only occurred in shifters. Not only wolves, but also mountain lions, and others. But I kept drinking and let Ollie tell the tale in his own way.

"Ah... I don't really believe you," Lexie said, then gulped. "But I'm also smart enough to know that I don't know shit about this world." She crossed her arms over her middle in a gesture that looked like self-protection. "Can you prove it?"

Ollie glanced over at me. "Mark?"

I groaned and got to my feet. Why not? I unbuttoned my shirt and kicked off my shoes. "If she freaks out or passes out, this is on you, Ollie."

I glanced at Lexie, who was staring at my bare chest. "You ready?"

She nodded. "Yes, please."

I sighed. "Okay. But number one, don't forget that I'm still me. I'm not going to bite you or attack you, or anything dumb, okay?"

Her mouth tightened, but she nodded again.

"And number two." I threw my shirt onto the couch next to Ollie, and prepared my wolf to rise up into my flesh. It wasn't difficult to call him forth as he was never far away, especially when Lexie was around. "Don't forget you asked for this."

CHAPTER 9
LEXIE

I wasn't sure why I was humoring these two. They were obviously insane. I should be running for the door, straight back to my tiny apartment and locking myself in tight.

But I didn't feel afraid. I couldn't explain it, but instead of fear, or annoyance at being lied to, a growing excitement deep inside me began to spread outward from my belly.

I suspected the feeling was amplified at the sight of Markus's naked chest.

Jeezus... wow.

Markus was a god. I'd never seen a man that sculpted, that perfect, that beautiful in real life.

But then, right before my eyes, he started to change. I kept blinking, trying to clear my vision, but it made no difference. His features became sharper, hairier, then he was shrinking in size. Down to the ground, on all fours like a... "Oh. My. *God.*"

I didn't move. I couldn't, even if I wanted to. Adrenaline zinged along my arms and legs, making my heart pound, but my butt seemed rooted to the spot. Would my suddenly shaking legs even hold me up if I jumped to my feet and tried to run? My gaze shot to the front door. Would I make it?

There was a wolf inside the house. A beautiful, terrifying *wolf*.

"Lexie? It's okay. It's still Markus. He won't hurt you, I promise. Lexie? Are you all right?" Ollie spoke from beside me, and I managed to turn and look at him, gulping down the fear that held my breath in tight.

"That's... Markus?"

I focused on Ollie, on the warmth of his gaze as he nodded and smiled gently. "It is. I promise you're safe."

"Um..." I glanced back at the wolf now sitting like a trained dog in the middle of the lounge room. Only, he was much larger than any dog I'd ever seen. "I... don't know what to do."

Ollie called out to the huge gray wolf. "Markus, shift back. I think she's got the picture."

The wolf stood, shook out its fur coat, and then the air around him seemed to waver and morph, until once again, Markus was there, standing before me in all his glory.

All his *naked* glory.

I couldn't help but stare at his long, thick cock, hanging against his thigh. A lick of arousal—which seemed so inappropriate given the circumstances—curled in my belly. He was absolutely magnificent, naked. Then he reached for his jeans and shirt, and the show was over.

I blinked and stood up, running my hands hurriedly through my hair. Had I imagined the whole thing?

Markus went to his part of the massive sofa and sat back down with his pizza and beer, as if nothing had happened.

I walked over to where the wolf had just been. Looked down at the carpet that had paw prints still softly embedded in the pile.

"I... did I just see a..." I didn't want to even say it.

I turned toward the two men. Ollie was still eating pizza and Markus was sipping a beer.

Markus shrugged. "Yes. We're wolves. No big thing."

"No. Big. Thing," I repeated, and began to pace. Up and down. My brain was finally clear and thinking fast. "So, you're telling me this is... normal. That there are lots of you guys?"

How was it possible that this secret had been kept quiet from most humans?

Markus grabbed a handful of peanut chocolate candies. "Yep. Nancy is part of our pack as well."

I crossed my arms over my boobs and glared down at him. "Oh my God. Don't tell me you're all skinny and fit and look like that."

Markus's lips flickered as though he was trying not to smile. "Most wolves are pretty fit, yeah. But no. They don't all look like us. Or her."

My temper flared, backed by a healthy dose of irrational jealousy.

"Well, if she's your type, what the hell am I doing here?" I threw up my hands and charged for the stairs. "I'll grab my shit and go home."

Markus got up and jumped in front of me faster than was humanly possible. *Oh, that's right. He isn't human.*

I glared at him. "What are you doing?"

"I'm—"

"What?" I put both hands on my hips. "You're going to lie and tell me you don't sleep with her?"

He shrugged. "I have in the past. So what? You going to tell me you're a virgin?"

Hell, no. I got rid of that *prize* at fifteen, as soon as I met a boy I liked. Being inexperienced and living with my mother in her den of danger, my virginity wasn't something I wanted stolen from me.

I'd been lucky.

But that wasn't the same as being a man-whore. "No... but..."

"No buts," he growled. "You have a past. I have a past. Hell, even perfect Ollie has a past. You don't get to hold that against me."

I inhaled sharply. Perfect Ollie? Sounded like he was holding onto a lot of shit, envy toward his brother being one of them.

"Beside the point," I countered. "How am I supposed to compete with women who look like Nancy?"

He rolled his eyes and groaned. "With women who have tight asses but no brain? Small boobs and no heart? Yeah... so much competition you have."

I was flabbergasted. Was he hinting that he was attracted to me, despite what I looked like? What was I supposed to say to that?

"Come back and we'll explain more," Ollie called from behind me. "Please."

If I was being completely honest, I had hoped that both of them might want me, at least a little bit. A massively arrogant hope, in retrospect. In reality, I had no right to be jealous of Nancy, or any other woman they had slept with.

I had no proof they even liked me at all, really.

Except for the way they had just jumped to stop me leaving.

I didn't understand what was going on. So, I turned around and stalked back to the only recliner chair in the room, separating myself from the guys. "Okay. Explain."

Markus indicated to Ollie, not speaking, and I had to assume he was giving his brother the stage.

Ollie slid forward, perching on the edge of the couch in a casual, far too sexy way.

"Look, this is gonna sound so strange to a human—"

"You mean, stranger than finding out you two can shift into wolves and back?"

He barked out a short laugh. "I guess that is strange to you. But there's more. Some of us in the various shifter packs are born as twins, called Perfect Pairs. We're opposite in every way—brains versus brawn, serious versus fun-loving, dark versus light. But our attributes complement each other, and legend has it that there is one person out there in the world who is designed just for us, as we are for her—our perfect mate. A Fated Mate. Like—"

"Like a soul mate?" I asked. "You guys have them for legit? Not like romance novel, movie bullshit?"

Markus jerked his head in a nod that was almost non-committal, so I focused on Ollie.

Ollie kept talking. "Yeah. When we meet the one Fated Mate meant for us, an electrical impulse literally takes our legs out from under us. It's the way it is with Fated Mates. The shock makes sure that we don't miss the perfect woman when we happen upon her."

Despite all the food I'd eaten this afternoon, my stomach began to feel hollow. Empty. Sick. *An electric impulse that takes their legs out from under them...*

"You can't be serious." They weren't saying that *I* was their... "For both of you? No way."

I couldn't believe it. I was so far from perfect, I simply couldn't be anyone's perfect soul mate. Let alone for two beautiful men like Ollie and Markus. There was just... "No. No."

I got up and began to pace and fidget at the same time. I would have looked crazy to an outsider, shaking my head about and twiddling my fingers, but I had so much nervous energy pulsing through me, I had no idea what to do with it all.

Ollie stood up but stayed close to the sofa, which I was glad about. I didn't want him crowding me. I was already feeling overwhelmed.

"For me?" he said. "Yes. It's true. Everything points to the fact that you're my mate. I've been waiting for you, and desperately want you to stay here. Be my partner in life."

I blew out an exasperated sigh. "You haven't even kissed me yet. How can you put so much faith into some electric, pulsing thing?"

Ollie's lips spread into a wide grin. "I can change that."

And before I could think about the challenge I'd thrown down, he stalked forward, slid his hand around my waist and pulled me into his body for a kiss.

My eyes slid closed as he took my mouth, pressing my lips apart and sweeping his tongue inside. I gasped and pushed closer, wrapping my arms around his neck and kissing him back with all the pent-up need inside of me.

He tasted divine, and the way his tongue danced with mine was like he'd kissed me a million times before.

I didn't stop kissing him, even with all the confusion and worry and grief I'd been through in the past. My old life was finished; I could feel it dropping away from me in the way a snake must feel when it sheds its skin. Slightly uncomfortable, but with relief and freedom following on swift wings.

I pressed against him harder, reaching for his shirt buttons. I wanted to feel his hot skin beneath my fingers. Explore the gorgeous body I knew was beneath his clothes.

But he pulled back, breathing hard. "Stop. We need to talk more. We have more to tell you."

I didn't want to talk. I didn't want to have it confirmed that Markus didn't want me. It was obvious he had issues up the wazoo. I'd had the shittiest few days—make that years—and I wanted to feel good for a while before my hopes were dashed yet again.

"Please," I whispered, undoing one button on his shirt, then the next.

Ollie's eyes flared with hunger. "You're not playing fair. You know how much I want you. You can probably feel it against you."

He thrust with his hips and the impressive erection I could, indeed, feel against my belly mashed even harder. More insistent. I gasped a little at the roll of heat that went through me, and he groaned. "Lexie."I went up on my toes and kissed him on the lips again. The fact that he wanted me so much and believed I was this amazing woman who had been designed just for him was fueling my need.

No one had ever declared they wanted me in such a way.

"What about Markus?" Ollie whispered against my mouth. "We need to talk about him. About what it all means."

I inhaled sharply and pulled back. I didn't know how to deal with Markus, but something told me that leaving him out now would be a huge error.

I pulled off the hoodie and tossed it onto the chair, then tiptoed over to Markus.

He was standing with his back against the wall, staring at me. His eyes were dark and troubled, blazing with a passion that appeared to be stoked by fury.

I tilted my head back and stared up at him. "You don't know what you want yet, do you?"

He didn't move to begin with, worry warring with the desire in his expression.

Then, at last, he shook his head.

I tried not to take offense. If anything, his honesty was refreshing. He wasn't trying to manipulate me into bed or lie about his intentions. What he was really saying was that he couldn't throw his hat into the ring like Ollie was. He couldn't commit to the whole idea about soul mates, and forever. Not yet anyway.

Anxiety filled my chest. What if he never could? My breath shortened, but I would not run away.

This was one of those life moments. I could sense it. A turning point, fucking important moment for all three of us. I could actually feel the depth and complexity of it, hanging like a heavy weight in the room. Invading my limbs and making the muscles tremble. Building fear in the pit of my stomach. Increasing the thumping of my heart against my ribs.

I took a deep breath and did the bravest thing I've ever done in my life. I pushed my jeans down my thighs and kicked out of my socks.

They're gonna think I'm fat. Totally unfuckable.

My t-shirt was long enough to cover my ass, thankfully, but that didn't stop my insecurities from rising like a high tide. I could feel my cheeks heating as my face burned with embarrassment. Had I just made a huge mistake? Had I given Markus a reason to run?

But Markus didn't seemed turned off. Quite the opposite, in fact. I'd never seen such a look of intense need as his gaze raked down my body and legs and back up again.

"Lexie... I don't.... I can't... the future..." He was trying to explain, I knew it. But I didn't need him to talk about forever.

"Let's put forever aside for now, Markus." My voice was husky. "What about right now?" I smiled at him, I hoped in a seductive way. "What about tonight?"

His pupils dilated and there was a flash of silver that had my breath catching in my throat. What *was* that? Was it his... wolf?

He made a strange, growly-type noise, then reached for me, sliding his hand under my t-shirt, to the bare skin at the base of my spine.

I whimpered as he pulled me against his body, the heat of his hand burning an imprint into my flesh.

He dropped his head and whispered into my ear. "I've never wanted anyone the way I want you, Lexie. You are the hottest... sexiest..." He nipped my ear with each punctuated word. "Woman I have ever seen. I can't think of anything better than sinking my cock into you."

I grabbed hold of his shirt and closed my eyes, needing the words as much as I needed his touch. Every syllable soothed years of injuries. A lifetime of rejection. Before now.

"But I don't want to hurt you," he whispered against my ear.

I slipped my hands down to his waistline and untucked his shirt. "No buts. Please. Just for tonight."

I knew it would break my heart if Markus decided he was kicking me to the curb after one night, but he and Ollie were worth the risk.

His mouth crashed down on mine, and everything around me faded away.

CHAPTER 10

LEXIE

I put everything I had in to kissing Markus. He groaned deep in his throat, then swept me up into his arms like I weighed nothing.

I squealed and fought him for a moment, clinging to his neck like a cat hanging over a bath. "Oh, put me down. Put me down. I'm too heavy."

But he just chuckled and said, "I bench press a hell of a lot more than you weigh, beautiful. We're taking this to the bedroom."

Ollie was on our heels as Markus jogged up the stairs.

Being held like this was a lesson in trust. I was terrified of being dropped, not really liking the feeling of being out of control. But tonight was about firsts in so many ways, and I was open to trying anything.

When we hit the landing, Markus took me down the hall to his room, then set me on my feet.

His room was dark and beautiful. Super masculine with a funky black shiplap feature wall, and large furniture.

Ollie stepped into the room behind us, his shirt still partially open. "I'm assuming I'm invited too?" His tone was slightly hesitant, and I turned my head and reached out my hand to him.

"Yes. Definitely," I said, looking between the twin brothers. "Though I have no idea..." My cheeks heated. "I've never been with more than one person at the same time before."

Ollie laughed and Markus smirked a little. "Well, funnily enough, we've never had sex with the same woman before," Markus said, "but I think we'll work it out."

A tiny part of my brain noted the fact that he didn't deny having a threesome, just that he hadn't shared a woman with Ollie.

I pushed the dark wisp of thought aside. These men were gorgeous, virile creatures, and their experiences were theirs to keep.

The past could stay in the past. It was the here and now that was important.

"Okay," I said, and smiled like an idiot, standing by the bed where Markus had deposited me. I was still in my t-shirt and underwear and felt sudden nerves that stopped me from completely stripping off.

Markus walked behind me, grabbed the edge of my top and lifted. "Arms up, Lexie."

I gulped down the threatening shriek that rose and lifted my arms, letting him strip me down to my underwear.

My panties were cotton, as was my bra. There weren't pretty bras for boobs my size, and I couldn't wait to get out of it.

I unclipped my bra and tossed it across the room. My boobs were heavy, but I did like their shape, and honestly, distracting the guys from my ugly underwear was key here.

They converged on me, Markus slipping his hands around my waist and sliding up, cupping both breasts with his warm hands. Ollie stepped forward, tracing around my jawline with an exploring finger before he drew me into him for a kiss. Markus pressed his lips to my neck and gave each of my nipples a squeeze.

I gasped at the dual sensual assault, which allowed Ollie to kiss me even deeper. Eventually he stopped and pulled away, but only briefly. He bent and tugged my underwear down my thighs. When it reached my feet, I kicked it away.

I was now naked, and both of them were still fully clothed. "This doesn't seem fair," I teased. "Can you guys strip too?"

Ollie stepped back and got out of his clothes so fast that he was naked before I had time to blink more than once or twice.

I drank in the view. Like Markus when he'd shifted back to his human form earlier, Ollie was gloriously beautiful in his nude state.

I gaped at his strength. His muscles. His beauty. "I can't believe two men who look like you, want someone who looks like me. Even for one night."

Ollie took a step forward and dropped to his knees in front of me. "Lexie, you're perfect. Quite literally. Everything about you is simply gorgeous."

Then he leaned forward and kissed my belly and I gasped. "Oh..." I kept my legs clamped together, not sure I was up for him exploring any lower with his mouth.

"Do you want to lie down?" he asked, raising an eyebrow. Even that action was sexy.

I nodded speechlessly, waiting for Markus to let go of my breasts, then scrambling onto the bed. My nerves were beginning to fail me in the face of... well, Ollie's face so near my pussy.

I pulled back the covers and jumped between the cool sheets but before I could drag them up to cover me, Ollie prowled over and grabbed hold of my ankles, sliding me out so I was lying on my back on top of the covers.

"We want to see you, beautiful," he growled, and began to crawl up between my legs, kissing the inside of my knees, then the soft inside of my thighs. I gasped, then moaned, at the exquisite sensation of his lips on my sensitized flesh.

Beside the bed Markus undressed too, and when I turned my head to look at him, my breath hitched in my throat.

His cock was no longer hanging soft and relaxed against his

thigh. Instead, it was thickening before my very eyes and rising up to declare his arousal.

I couldn't resist the allure. "I'm just gonna shuffle over a little, okay?" I said to Ollie, moving closer to the edge of the bed before twisting so that my head was close to Markus.

He grinned down at me. "Did you move over here for me?"

I had to laugh. "Would there be another reason I'd be on this level?" Then I did the boldest thing I'd ever done and opened my mouth for him.

His eyes flared then he grabbed his cock in one hand and fed the head into my mouth.

The moment my lips wrapped around his beautiful, thick cock, Ollie's tongue slid over my clit.

I cried out, the sound muffled by Markus's thick dick between my lips.

Oh my God!

The sensations were incredible. I reached one hand down to find Ollie, threading my fingers through his soft hair, while my other hand was wrapped around the largest male appendage I'd ever seen.

I sucked on the head of Markus's cock, silk over steel, salty and perfect, loving the fact that I was making him groan above my head.

Ollie's tongue and mouth on me were heaven sent. He flicked my clit over and over, the warmth of his breath adding to the pleasure, pushing my desire higher and higher.

I came off Markus's cock to pant, unable to breathe and moan and suck at the same time.

Markus stepped away, crawling onto the bed to lie beside me.

"Oh... ah..." I gasped and moaned, my belly clenching tight.

Markus set his lips to one of my nipples and his fingers tweaked the other.

I closed my eyes and groaned. I couldn't think. It was too much.

I had a hand on each of the men—my men—and I couldn't believe how connected I felt. How right this was. How perfect.

My eyes opened, my stress level rising at the idea of my perfect pair and everything they needed.

But at that same moment, Markus pushed up on his hands and kissed me. Hard. And Ollie slid his fingers inside me, ratcheting my pleasure up to the point of no return.

I shattered into a massive orgasm, crying out into Markus's mouth while Ollie remained clamped on the sensitive flesh between my legs.

My back arched as the spasms hit my belly, my nails digging into Ollie's head.

When my orgasm tremors began to ebb away, I collapsed onto the mattress, and tears began leaking down the sides of my face. I couldn't make them stop.

I lifted my hands to cover my face. "I'm sorry." I kept sobbing and laughing, unable to stop the hot tears as they continued to roll down my face.

Markus was silent but slid his hand onto my belly in a gesture that felt protective.

Ollie slid up the bed on my other side and took my chin in his fingers. He turned my face toward him. "Baby girl... what's wrong? Why are you crying?"

"I... I..." I curled toward him, pressing my forehead to his chest while I wept.

I couldn't believe I could feel so good, so cared for. That was as big a shock to my system as the pleasure I'd just experienced.

I'd never had an orgasm with a man before, and I just couldn't even process all the feelings.

"I'll go," Markus said, and I had to stop him.

I rolled over and on top of him, pushing him back down. "No. Stay."

Markus lay back down, but his eyebrows were low and his hands were clenched on the mattress.

I wiped the tears from my cheeks and Ollie handed me a tissue. I blew my nose and mopped up my face, then pulled myself together. "Okay, I'm sorry. That was not what you think it was."

Markus didn't move, but he said, "It looked like you were devastated."

"No. I was…" I stared up at the ceiling, then down at my huge man. "Overwhelmed, in every way."

I placed both hands on his chest, leaning forward so my hair fell forward and my breasts swung a little.

Markus's hands slid up onto my thighs, but I knew I needed to explain. "I've never had an orgasm like that before."

"You mean with two men working on you?" Ollie asked, sliding closer.

I laughed. "No… I mean… I've never had an orgasm. *Ever*."

"You're fucking with us." Markus's tone was shocked.

I laughed at his flabbergasted expression; I couldn't help it. "No. I mean… I might have had one… once or twice by… me. But nothing like that. And definitely never with another person. I didn't know I could feel like that. You two just blew me away. Completely."

Markus glanced over at Ollie.

Then Ollie said, "So you liked it? They weren't *sad* tears?"

I covered my face again, this time to cover the laughter. "Of course, I did! And no, they weren't sad tears at all. They were oh-my-fucking-god-I'm-insanely-happy tears."

Ollie sat up and moved forward until he was close enough to kiss me. He stopped just above me, his lips hovering enticingly close to mine. "So… do you wanna keep going?"

I leaned forward to close the distance between us and kissed him, tasting myself on his lips. My insides lurched with excitement. "Absolutely."

CHAPTER 11

MARKUS

I gripped Lexie's thighs, loving the thickness beneath my fingers. The strength. The lushness of her whole body. She had something to grab onto, and I was already envisioning how much fun it would be to pound her into the mattress.

I'd be able to give her my full weight and not be afraid to hurt her. What a relief that would be.

My gaze traveled up her body, resting on her beautiful pink nipples. Her breasts were huge, and I couldn't wait to get my hands and my mouth on them again.

As she leaned forward to kiss Ollie, I gave in to temptation and reached up, filling my hands with her warm flesh and thumbing over her peaked nipples.

Lexie gasped and arched her back, pushing her breasts even harder into my hands.

I kneaded her flesh, loving how different she was from every other woman I'd touched before. Somehow it made her so much more special. I'd never forget this moment. Then she began to move, gyrating her hips over my cock before throwing one of her legs over my hips to press even more firmly against my erection.

I'd gone from almost ready to come when she'd orgasmed, to completely flaccid when she'd begun to cry. My heart had sunk at the thought of her sadness. Never in my life had I wanted to hold a woman while she sobbed—until Lexie. But I had no idea what to do to help her, so when she curled into Ollie, I'd simply clenched my fists to stop from touching her.

I'd felt useless, and worse... rejected.

But now she was on top of me, and clearly hot for what I had to give her. My cock swelled into full arousal faster than it ever had before, as her dripping pussy rubbed along the shaft.

I could scent her need perfuming the air around us, and it excited me almost beyond control.

I gripped her hips and lifted her. "Lexie, take me inside you."

She stopped kissing Ollie and pushed up on her knees.

I grabbed my cock and moved it up and down her seam. She was so wet and I was dripping with pre-cum. I painted her pussy lips with our combined wetness and she trembled a little at my action. I couldn't hold out any longer.

I positioned the shaft so that the head was nudging open her entrance and held myself still beneath her. She lifted up, looked down at me, then slid straight down on top of me, taking me in as if we were made for each other. I dismissed that thought, groaning as she took every inch of my cock, then she threw her head back with a gasp. "Oh!" she cried. "That feels so damn good, Markus!"

"Damn, you're so hot. So tight." I clenched my jaw hard, trying not to come from a single thrust. Sex had never felt like this before. So electric and intense. So right and out of control at the same time.

Her pussy was perfect. Wet and tight, my cock slid right in and up inside her like he was finding *home*. Another thought I dismissed as soon as it appeared.

When she finally began to rock on me, I couldn't stay still. I planted my feet on the bed, grabbed her hips and began thrusting upward.

"Oh… ah… Oh…" Lexie moaned and gasped, pressing her hands against my chest and rotating her hips so she could ride me properly.

I filled my palms with her breasts again and met each of her downward thrusts with one of my own.

Staring up at Lexie on top of me, my mind captured every moment like a camera snapping pictures of her beauty. Every gasp. Every writhe and pleasurable expression on her face.

She was fucking beautiful. The sexiest woman I'd ever seen, and knowing that she'd never had an orgasm with anyone else made me rock hard.

But despite the fact that she looked beautiful on top of me, I had to change our position. My wolf and I wanted her beneath us.

"I'm going to roll over with you," I growled, grabbing her hips to hold her in place and flipping her until she was under me.

She squealed as we rolled, then gasped as I thrust deep inside her.

I wasn't normally one for the classic missionary position. I usually felt smothered, too close to the other person, or something. But I wanted Lexie right there, in my face, her breasts pressed against my chest as I sunk my cock into her pussy.

She grabbed my biceps as I drove into her, then wrapped her legs around my waist.

I reached back and grabbed one of her thighs, pushing her leg higher, opening her even wider. I wanted to hit that sweet spot inside her. Make her scream for me this time.

Her eyes widened as her lips fell open, "Oh… my…"

I'd found it, and watching shock and pleasure fill her face, I couldn't hold back any longer.

I pounded into her over and over again, her screams of pleasure filling my ears, her nails digging into my arms, her pussy clamping down so hard on my cock it was like she was trying to squeeze it off.

Heat tingled in my balls and spread up my back and down the backs of my legs. I was going to blow. There was no stopping it now.

I set my lips to Lexie's neck, inhaling her scent into my senses before I thrust one last time. I came deep inside her, freezing in place to pump her as full as I could.

Fireworks exploded inside my mind and for a single moment, there was no sound, no breath, no world. Only the woman in my arms, wrapped around me, holding me in a way I'd never experienced before.

Close. Tight.

She pulled me up to her for a kiss, our lips meeting, and a shiver of electricity worked its way through me.

I moaned at the pleasure and rolled us to the side, so I didn't squash her when I collapsed onto the mattress.

She was panting as I withdrew, and she rested her hand over my heart. Every touch, every look sent a little shock of electricity through me.

Mate. Mate. Mate, my wolf chanted inside my head.

I closed my eyes. I didn't want to think about what that word would mean for me. For Ollie. For our future.

Ollie slid onto the bed behind Lexie and ran a hand around her waist, cupping her breast from behind. She turned her head toward him, capturing his lips in a kiss.

When she bumped her hips back at him, inviting him in an age-old mating move, Ollie slid down the mattress a little, lined up and thrust into Lexie from behind.

She groaned as he penetrated deep, then gasped as he began to move. He was gripping her hips, his fingers sinking into the luscious flesh of her hips. Her eyes were squeezed shut, but she was clearly in rapture.

I glanced over at the door. I wasn't sure what I should do. Stay? Go have a shower? I felt awkward and uncertain.

I rolled onto my back, so I wasn't staring at them anymore. I weighed up my options. Stay or go? Ollie had stayed and watched me fuck Lexie. I should return the favor, and I couldn't leave now. I'd ruin the whole atmosphere of the room.

Lexie cried out suddenly, her hands grabbing at my arm. "Markus! Kiss me. Please."

Ollie was fucking her fast now and I could see it in her eyes that she was about to come again.

I rolled over to her, getting as close as I could without impeding what was going on.

She lurched for me, meeting my lips with her own and kissing me hard.

When I opened my mouth and slid my tongue inside her lips, she opened on a gasp, then sucked hard on my tongue.

I cupped her face with my hands, sipping from her lips until she cried out and began to shudder.

A wave of pleasure washed over me as she came again. Instead of being distracted by my own orgasm, I got to hold her close and revel in my woman's happiness.

Since I was young, I'd wondered how this would feel, to watch my brother loving on my mate. I'd fought the idea, denying that we'd ever fall for the same girl. But the concept had lingered and remained at the edge of my worries for over a decade.

And here we were, in bed with the woman we'd both experienced the Fated Mate attraction with. I wasn't feeling sick, repulsed or on edge. I wasn't consumed with rage, or jealousy. Instead, my focus was on Lexie and how much pleasure she was receiving. And it felt fucking *awesome*. Why would I ever withhold that pleasure from her? Especially if that was Fate's design—for Lexie to have two men.

Ollie finished soon after and we were all left panting, sweaty and in a cuddle that I couldn't have left if my life depended on it.

Ollie withdrew and Lexie moved closer to me, resting her head on my chest as she continued to shiver with the aftermath of her orgasms.

I lay on my back with my head on the pillow, Lexie in my arms. I pressed a kiss to her hair and held her tightly, happiness like nothing I'd ever felt raining down on me.

My brother sat up, then pulled the blankets up over us and settled on the other pillow behind her.

It was time to sleep, and I wasn't letting Lexie go.

I glanced over at my twin and an unspoken understanding passed between us.

The electricity pulses had been right. Ollie had been right. I had been wrong.

She was my mate. Our mate. Shit.

What was I going to do now?

CHAPTER 12

LEXIE

I woke up to a kiss being pressed against my cheek. "Good morning, beautiful."

Ollie hovered over me, dressed in a crisp white shirt and gray suit. "Hi," was all I managed, both struck by his beauty and still below the sleep cloud. Even opening my eyes was a challenge.

"I'm heading to work, but Markus will be here for lunch. I'll be home as soon as I can tonight. Okay?"

I nodded against the pillow and mumbled, "Sounds great," then passed out again.

The next time I woke up it was to a still, quiet house. "Hello?" I called out, sitting up in Markus's massive bed and stretching my arms above my head.

Waking up naked was strange, feeling the sheets and blankets brushing against my bare skin. I'd never slept completely naked before, without even a tank or a pair of panties.

My body ached, too, but in a wonderful way, every move reminding me of the mind-blowing sex and the orgasms that had torn through my body.

I slid out of bed, grabbed a skirt and a top along with some underwear out of my duffel bag and bolted to the bathroom. It was strange to think that I didn't have to go to work today. I'd always had a job, sometimes juggling two or three. I believed in earning my way in this world.

The very idea that I could just live in this beautiful house rent-free felt, well... wrong. I'd call around today and start looking for a new job immediately. I wanted to be able to pay my way.

The shower beckoned and I stepped into the huge space. I smelled of my men, which was a combination of sweat and sex. The scent had me faintly aroused all over again, and I chuckled as I turned on the water and then covered my face with my hands while I waited for the heat to adjust, even though there was no one here to see my embarrassed blush.

I'd had sex with two men. *At the same time.* I couldn't get over it.

And how was I supposed to process the whole shifter-animal thing? That was insane! But I'd seen it with my own eyes. I shook my head again and stepped beneath the spray, letting the hot water run down my back.

I didn't know where to start with all the strange things I'd discovered yesterday.

There were too many unknowns surrounding my relationship with Markus and Ollie, if it could even be called that after only a couple of days. But I was too happy to worry about such unknowns at the moment. I wanted to enjoy these rare minutes of bliss without having to think about all the obstacles that were in our way.

Fated Mates.

Markus not wanting a mate at all.

Me not being a shifter.

Them *being* shifters. Wolves!

This was all absolutely crazy.

"Stop it!" I told myself, scrubbing my body clean, then hopping out to dry myself.

I may not have currently had a job, but I was determined to make myself useful for them today. Clean the house, make some dinner maybe. I hadn't even seen most of the house.

I dressed in the relaxed t-shirt and a long boho skirt I'd pulled out of my bag, enjoying the new sensations making me more aware of my body than usual. The slight ache between my thighs, my swollen nipples. The dreamy, almost intoxicated state of my head.

I meandered downstairs, loving the feel of the soft carpet beneath my bare feet as I made my way to the kitchen. There, on the large marble island counter, was a handwritten note.

Markus's cell number...

Oliver's cell number... and work line...

Enjoy the day. Watch TV. Sunbathe. Whatever suits you. And we'll be home ASAP.

P.S. We don't have your cell number yet, and we need it.

I smiled at the note, then walked to the fridge. I wasn't particularly hungry, but when I saw the tub of creamy blueberry yogurt, I had to scoop some into a bowl.

Then I sat on the couch, put the TV on, and watched a selling houses lifestyle show for half an hour.

It was so decadent, so lazy. I kept glancing around, waiting for the dream to end. For someone to come along and catch me being bad. This had to be wrong somehow, surely?

The house was insanely clean. I wasn't sure if the guys had a housekeeper or were just rare men who were house proud and kept it neat themselves, but the carpet was vacuumed, the kitchen spotless. And there wasn't a thing out of place.

It wasn't very homey. There weren't any pictures on the walls, or even pillows on the sofa. Minimal. Masculine.

But truly lovely.

There was a knock on the front door, and I jumped. According to the large clock on the wall it was only ten-thirty. Would Markus be back already? What time did he start work in the morning?

And if it was him, he wouldn't knock, surely?

The front door opened, and a woman's voice sung out. "Hello? Is anyone here?"

I gulped. Who the hell was that? Their housekeeper, maybe?

I peeked around the corner and into the living room, not sure who I was about to meet.

A woman in her fifties stared back at me. She was slim and strong looking, with shoulder-length gray hair and dark eyes very similar to Markus's. "Hello," she said, studying me intently.

"Ah... hello," I answered, stepping into the lounge room.

"You must be my sons' new mate."

My jaw dropped for a moment before I pulled myself together and rushed over to her. "You're Markus and Ollie's mom? It is so nice to meet you. I've heard great things about you."

I held my hand out to shake, but she opened her arms and came forward for a hug.

When she engulfed me in her embrace, I hugged her back, though a little stiffly, I was sure. I wasn't used to the happy family vibe. I'd always made myself as invisible as possible when I was growing up, glad if my mom and her biker friends forgot I existed.

When she finally pulled back, I said, "I was just about to make a cup of tea. Would you like one too?"

"Of course. But allow me, I know my way around this kitchen. Probably better than you." She charged ahead, putting on the kettle and taking cups and things out of various cupboards.

I followed, wondering if she'd meant to be slightly offensive, then shaking it off. Of course, she hadn't meant anything by the comment. It was true. This was her sons' home and she *would* know their kitchen better than me. I slid onto the stool at the edge of the island. "I'm Lexie, by the way."

"Anne," she said, and this time I noticed that her smile didn't quite reach her eyes. "What do you do, Lexie?"

I hated that question, but I answered honestly enough. "Do for what? A job? I'm a waitress, mostly." What I did to pay my rent didn't define who I was. Quite the opposite.

"Because you're studying? At which college?" Her assumption that hospitality was only an in-between job seemed a bit elitest and made me instantly uncomfortable.

I glanced down at the counter, staring at the gray veins running through the marble. "Ah... no. I didn't finish high school. I didn't even try to get into college."

Anne pushed a teacup over the counter toward me. I picked it up and took a sip.

She wasn't speaking, and I wasn't sure what else to say. Then it occurred to me that she shouldn't know about me yet. I'd only met the guys thirty-six hours ago and as far as I know they hadn't told their mom about me.

My head came up and I studied the woman whose lips were twisted into a strange pinch. "Did Ollie call you and ask you to check up on me?"

She tilted her head. "No. Why would you ask that?"

"Oh, I was just wondering how you knew your sons had found their... ah... mate." It was still strange using that word and didn't yet roll easily off my tongue.

Anne shifted her weight, standing a little straighter. "I ran into Nancy last night and she informed me that Ollie had declared you were his mate. In Walmart, of all places."

I smiled in memory. "Yeah, I had no idea what he was saying at the time, but Ollie asked me to play along, so I did."

Anne leveled me with the intensity of her next look. "But you understand now?"

I shivered at the strangely veiled threat beneath her words. "If you mean about the perfect pairs and the wolf stuff. Yes."

"Wolf. Stuff," she repeated, spitting out each word. "I can't believe they told you. The council won't be happy."

I took another sip of my tea. She didn't seem to be asking me a question; she was just muttering to herself.

Her eyes flashed silver, then she said, "You're human. You have no concept of nor respect for what we are."

My jaw dropped and I put my teacup down. "That's not fair," I managed, my temper beginning to ignite. This woman had clearly meant to be offensive, right from the moment she walked in.

"I found out about the existence of shifters last night. Like..." I glanced at the clock. "Sixteen hours ago."

"Oh... you can do basic math. How quaint."

I gaped at her, shocked at the rudeness of the woman who had raised my men to be such wonderful people. "What is your problem?"

"My problem is that I expected the woman my sons chose to be up to their level. In intelligence, beauty, and family connections. I have to assume that you don't have parents watching over you, helping you?"

I shook my head. "No. I don't." Quite the opposite.

She nodded once. "Just as I thought. You're not good enough for my boys."

"Your... boys?" I repeated, narrowing my eyes at the nasty woman who'd officially ruined my day. "Those boys are men. And as far as I understand, this Fated Mate electric, pulsey thing doesn't make mistakes."

Anne didn't respond verbally. She paled and froze like I'd shocked her with something.

I crossed my arms over my chest and waited for another fireball to come out of her mouth.

"You experienced the Fated mate sign?" She gulped.

I stood up and put my hands on the counter, leaning forward to spear her with my look. "With both of your sons, yes. They were knocked right off their feet." Part of me enjoyed the momentary horror that crossed Anne's features, so I added, "Do you think I'd be here in their house if we hadn't experienced that? Ollie fell sideways and into a store on Main Street. Markus literally keeled over and hit the deck, right over there near the fridge." I pointed to the floorboards near her feet, and Anne took a big step back.

Then she turned and began heading toward the front door, like a zombie. "I have to go."

I followed her because how could I not? She'd just burst into the house to tell me I wasn't good enough for either of her sons. As if I already didn't know that! But I didn't appreciate someone else pointing it out in such a rude way.

"What were you expecting?" I called out to her. "That they'd just randomly choose some human they've never met before, and call her their mate?"

I couldn't believe I was being so forceful. I was the one who hadn't believed them when they'd told me about the soul mate stuff. But here I was, practically yelling at a woman who could probably rip me to shreds if she so chose.

Anne opened the front door and turned around. "What does Markus think about all this?"

"By 'all this', I assume you mean me and the human mate thing?" And why was she only asking about Markus and not about Ollie?

Anne frowned, the edge of her mouth turning down along with her brows. "Markus isn't a monogamous male. Never has been, never will be. I don't think... I don't know if he can have one mate like a normal member of a perfect pair triad."

I stared her down. "Well, that's really up to him and me, isn't it? But thanks for the tip."

I was spitting venom now. *Fucking bitch.*

Anne walked out without shutting the door behind her, so I grabbed the handle and slammed the door as loudly as I could.

The sound ricocheted through the house, but my anger still bubbled too strong to contain. My hands tightened into fists, and I screamed out in frustration.

That's when the door opened again, only this time Markus came running in. "What's happened? Lexie! Are you okay?"

I marched up to him, not sure if I was going to hit him or kiss him. Neither, as it turned out.

Instead, I started yelling. "Am I okay? No! I am not okay! Your mother decided to pop in, thanks to your fuck friend Nancy!"

"Mom? What did she have to say?"

"She said I'm not good enough for her sons!"

"She fucking *what*?" His eyes flashed with silver, a trait I was noticing coincided with his lust as well as anger.

I began to pace the plush carpet, throwing my hands around with my words. "She said I'm not smart enough. Not pretty enough. Too human for you. And that you'll never be satisfied with one woman. Especially me, I guess, with all my failings. Well, I *know* I'm not good enough for you guys, okay? I already told Ollie that! I'm sorry, all right? I'm sorry I'm human. I'm sorry I'm fat. I'm sorry I'm dumb."

Markus grabbed me and hauled me up against his huge, hard body. "Stop talking like that. It's not true."

"Your own mother said it, Markus!"

His hands tightened on my hips and my pussy ached for him, which made me even angrier. What was it about this man that made me need him so much? "She said you're not monogamous, that you'll never be monogamous. Not even to a woman you think is your mate."

Markus turned us around, then pressed me up against the door, my spine against the wood.

"She doesn't know what she's talking about," he ground out, hissing the words out.

His hands were moving now, down my thighs and grabbing at my long skirt, bunching it up around my waist.

My body throbbed at the prospect of more sex with one of my gorgeous men, but my mind was angry and wanted answers. "Oh, really?" I demanded.

"Yes really," he said, his words brushing against my lips. "Is she right that I've always fucked who I want, when I want? Yes."

"Then how is this different?" I panted as he slipped his fingers between my thighs and began stroking my clit through my underwear.

"How?" he repeated. "You're my mate. That's how. It changes everything."

"But you don't want it to."

"I don't know!"

I had so many more questions, but as he brushed aside my underwear to slide a finger inside me, all the words in my head evaporated and I was only left with feeling.

I grabbed his shirt and hauled him closer, smashing my mouth against his. Our kiss was aggressive and so hot, it burned through me like a brush fire. I whimpered as he thrust his finger deeper, stoking the flame of desire while making me ache for more.

My tongue searched for his, sliding into his mouth while my hands went to the waistband of his jeans, opening his belt and tearing open the buttoned fly.

Markus groaned into my mouth when I released his cock and wrapped my hand around the thick, hot shaft.

He pulled back just long enough for me to push my underwear and my skirt to the floor, then he lifted me up against the door and impaled me with his cock.

I cried out at every possessive thrust, clinging to him, biting his neck, wanting to get closer. Needing more. Needing it harder. Faster.

He seemed to know what I craved, though neither of us spoke. He just nailed me again and again, fucking me through one orgasm that rolled into the next.

On my third belly-tightening, star-spinning orgasm that made me clench tightly and convulse against him, he came too.

This time he roared loudly in my ear, and I sank my teeth down into the flesh of his shoulder, relishing in the strong streams of heat that filled my belly.

I kissed his face, his lips, his throat. Anywhere I could reach, wanting him to know how much I needed him. How amazing he was.

The silence stretched as our breathing slowly returned to normal.

"Are you okay?" Markus whispered against the side my face.

I nodded. "I'm more than okay."

He withdrew, and I winced at the tenderness of the flesh that had received more male attention this past twenty-four hours than it ever had.

I reached for my underwear and skirt, dressing again as Markus re-buttoned and fixed up his shirt that I'd managed to crinkle to the point of no return.

"Ah... I'm sorry about that. Taking you so roughly." He was staring at the floor and seemed genuinely worried that he'd taken me against my will for some reason.

Far from it.

I smiled at my big, gruff guy. "Oh, please don't be sorry. Take me like that anytime you want."

His head came up and he stared straight at me. "You liked it?"

I laughed. "Um... You couldn't feel me coming around you? Over and over again?"

"Well, yeah, but..." He grinned and walked the few steps over to me and kissed me again, but this time with a hint of gentleness in his touch. "You really are perfect, aren't you?"

I let him drag me back to bed for a cuddle before he said he had to return to work and I dozed off into sleep once more.

My body was sated but my heart was in turmoil. No matter how awful she'd been, maybe Anne was right. Would Markus ever be able to love me the way I knew I could love him? And where did that leave Ollie? If they came as a so-called perfect pair, would it work if only one of the pair accepted me?

Time was the only thing that would tell.

CHAPTER 13

MARKUS

I didn't go back to work. I texted the guys to say I had to sort out a family issue, and instead, went and saw the diner owner that Lexie used to work for.

Despite the amazing sex we'd enjoyed—or perhaps because of it, with my body and emotions in heightened mode—I was full of testosterone and rage.

At my mom.

At Fate.

At every person who'd told me that I was a shit of a man and didn't have the heart or discipline to be a decent husband.

So, instead of staying with the woman I was meant to mate with, I left and drove into town. I was there in mere minutes and found a parking spot right out the front of the diner.

It was early in the week, and mid-afternoon, so Main Street was quiet at this time.

I hopped out of the truck and tightened my belt another hole. I hadn't tightened it properly after sex with Lexie, being too concerned about her.

Damn, that session had been hot.

Last night had been amazing enough, but to come home and be able to turn her anger into a way to connect and be close... that had been incredible. To take her so roughly against the wall had satisfied every urge inside me, and while I'd hoped she enjoyed it too, the moment we were done I'd begun to worry. What if she hadn't enjoyed it? What if she hated it, and was disgusted with how I'd just treated her? I'd immediately assumed she would turn away. Be horrified at my animal impulses.

More than one lover in the past had complained about my passion, especially human women. It was one of the reasons I preferred sleeping with shifters. They didn't look down on me for needing a bit of roughness, or tell me I'd gone too far and pushed them past their comfort level.

It made the tenderness Lexie showed me afterwards so much sweeter, knowing she accepted every part of me.

When I'd carried her to bed because she looked like she was half asleep on her feet, she'd wanted to cuddle, to kiss. To touch my face and whisper how wonderful our time together had been.

Such a stark contrast to the wildcat who had been in my arms only minutes before.

And damn, I loved both sides of her, equally.

I shook off the distracting thought, though the feeling of warmth toward Lexie remained. A perfect pair like Ollie and me were complimentary, but also significantly different men.

I'd always believed it would be impossible to find a woman who would suit both of us and yet, Lexie seemed to have all the fire I required, coupled with a tender and sweet side that calmed me. How she suited Ollie as well, I had no idea, but he seemed just as rapt with her as I was.

I rolled up my shirt sleeves while I leaned against my truck and stared up at the sign above the diner. If the owner was in, he was paying Lexie her money.

We didn't need the cash, of course, but she'd earned it. And I had the feeling she'd be one of those women who didn't want to take unnecessarily from others but needed her own money. More power to her, if she did.

I walked forward and pushed open the glass door, the bells ringing above my head.

"Hey. Take a seat and I'll be with you in a minute." The waitress behind the counter smiled at me.

I walked up to the seats at the counter. "I'm looking for the owner."

The girl frowned as though that was an unusual request. "He's not working today. Can I leave him a message?"

I leaned forward to put my hands on the counter. "No. But I do need to speak to him. Can you tell me when he'll be in next?"

She stared at me quizzically, as if trying to figure me out. "Can I ask what this is about?"

How much could I trust her? "Do you know Lexie at all?"

The girl's face transformed, lighting up with a huge smile. "Oh, yeah. She's awesome. I can't believe the boss fired her for punching some guy who was handsy with her. We get treated like shit and no one cares."

"I care," I managed to growl out. "And I want to sort out a few things with your boss."

She looked left and right as though to make sure no one else was listening. Then she dropped her voice to a whisper and said, "He's in tomorrow. Dinner shift. Five till eleven."

I winked at her and gave her a smile that I usually reserved for someone I was trying to seduce. "Thanks."

Then I left. The girl was cute, but she was young, and my wolf wasn't interested in her. Not one bit.

I frowned as I climbed into my truck. She'd definitely been cute. And not *that* young. My disinterest was a strange reaction.

My phone buzzed, and when I glanced down there was a text from Nancy.

You coming over tonight?

My immediate response was a loud groan. *Hell, no.*

I blinked. Since when did I knock back Nancy? Was I seriously cured from feeling like I needed to be on the hunt all the time? Never satisfied. Was the feeling actually gone?

I had to test out this strange theory.

I texted back. *I'm busy tonight, but can catch up for a drink now. You around?*

Nancy was a sales consultant and could be anywhere in the city at any time.

Yeah. I'm around the corner from my place. You wanna come over for a beer?

In Nancy speak that was, "Do you wanna come by for a quick fuck?" And maybe I did… I wanted to see what my wolf would do if I gave him the option.

I sent back, *Cool. Be there in ten.*

During the drive to Nancy's townhouse, my gut twisted tighter with every quarter mile that passed. When I finally pulled up outside her place and saw the lights in the window, I couldn't get out of the truck.

I tried to. I told myself I wanted to, even if I wasn't sure I did. I sure as hell didn't want to sit there like a stuffed turkey. But my legs wouldn't move. My arms wouldn't reach for the door handle.

My wolf remained curled up inside my chest, unmoving.

"Come on. Get out. She's waiting." With a cold beer and a hot pussy. "You pussy. Move!"

But there was no use. It appeared I was paralyzed from the neck down. Frozen in place.

"Fine," I grunted out. "Let's go home." Then suddenly I was able to turn the key and start the truck again.

I couldn't help but laugh. "You idiot." And the funniest part of all was that my wolf was also happy to go home, giving a rumble of approval before curling up once again to sleep. He suddenly didn't want anything to do with a woman I'd had hundreds of times during the past decade.

And neither did I.

Nancy came running out the front door with a huge smile on her face and the door to my escape slammed shut on me. "You're here! Come inside."

I turned the ignition off again and got out. I already had my answer, I didn't need to go inside. But Nancy and I had a lot of history and the last thing I wanted to do was insult her. We had a better friendship than that. Or so I thought.

The front door was open, so I went inside.

She shut the door behind us.

"Beers are on the counter!" she called out as I walked through the living room, familiar with the layout. I'd been here more times than I could count.

I wasn't sure exactly how I was going to explain that I was off the market, but it had to be said.

I found the beers and grabbed one, taking a sip to quench my thirst. I really needed water. The session with Lexie had really dehydrated me.

I wanted to go home to Lexie. I still wasn't sure whether I wanted a mate and all that went with it, but I wanted her. And that was a start.

Nancy sauntered into the room naked, her tiny tits pushed out.

I groaned and closed my eyes. "Nancy. Stop."

"Stop what?" she asked, grabbing onto my shirt and pushing the buttons through the holes at lightning speed.

I twisted away to stop her and put the beer back down on the counter. "I came here for a drink and a chat."

Nancy folded her arms over her breasts and affected a powerful stance. Her pussy was shaved, her body sleek and strong. And not a single hair on my wolf stirred to look her way.

If anything, I was feeling sicker by the minute. Guilty. I shouldn't be here.

Wow. You've got it bad.

"I've gotta go."

I went to walk past her. I wasn't sticking around to deal with this. She stepped in my way and pushed her hand against my chest. "Don't tell me this is because of that fat little human I saw with Ollie last night?"

I growled at her, a clear warning and one her wolf wouldn't ignore.

She snapped her trap shut but continued to glare at me.

"Get out of my way, Nancy."

"You can't be serious!" she said. "You're not Ollie. You don't want a mate for life. Or little brats hanging around your ankles. We've already talked about this a hundred times. You could never be faithful to a woman you have to share. This whole perfect pair shit is fucked up."

They were the same words I'd said a thousand times to anyone who would listen. They were the same thoughts I'd expressed to her since we were twenty years old.

Yet hearing my words come out of her luscious, poisonous mouth, they sounded wrong. I didn't believe them anymore.

My glare made her take a step back. "Nance. Get out of the way. I'm going home to Lexie. I don't know if she'll be my mate, or what's happening there, but you and I are done. You need to find another fuck friend."

I walked around her and left the house, shuddering at the dirty feeling I had all over my body. Was this what it felt like to be content? To be happy with the woman I was with?

I'd never known this feeling before. Even on nights where I'd had sex—hell, even a threesome with two hot women—it didn't stop me looking for the next one as soon as we were done. I was never satisfied, the heat in my blood never quenched. But as I drove home to my house on the outskirts of town, my wolf slept happily.

I'd truly never known such peace.

When I pulled up outside the house, my phone rang, and I answered. It was my dad.

"Markus. Your mother and I need to have a word."

"Now?" I asked, turning off the ignition and leaning back in the seat. I was finally home. Couldn't it wait?

"Preferably. Can you come right away?"

I frowned. "What about Ollie?" My parents never spoke to us separately, especially not about anything important.

"We just need to speak to you. If you're free, come by."

"I'm free," I confirmed, aching to go inside, but feeling like my parents' fears needed addressing. Mom had already upset Lexie once. I didn't want her doing it again.

"We're home," Dad said.

So I started the truck once more and set off, hoping that Lexie had found something to occupy her afternoon, because I was learning more about myself today than I ever thought possible. And I couldn't wait to get back to her.

CHAPTER 14

LEXIE

When there was another knock on the door, I raced for it. Was it Ollie? Or had Markus come home again?

I missed them, and I wanted to tell them about the interviews I had lined up for this week. I may not be a college graduate, and Anne would probably never like me, but at least their wolf shifter family and friends would never be able to say that I sponged off the twins.

The last person I expected to see on the other side of the door was the bitch from Walmart.

"Oh, hello," I managed, wishing I could just slam the door in her face. But from what Ollie had said, Nancy wasn't just Markus's lover, she was a family friend. And the last thing I needed to do was offend someone else.

She grinned at me like the cat who ate the cream, though in this regard it was more like the wolf who ate the girl. "I just wanted to drop this off. Is Markus home yet?" She waved a credit card or something in my face.

I didn't move back or open the door any further. I wasn't letting her in.

"No, he's not. You can give it to me." I held out my hand, and to my surprise, she dropped the card in my palm without a fight. "Ah... thanks."

"Markus left my place about half an hour ago, so he shouldn't be too far away," she said, glancing around as though she was expecting him home any moment. "I think the card fell out of his pocket when he took his pants off... or something."

He fucking what?

I stared at her, not sure I'd heard her correctly. Surely, she was just here to be nasty. "You must be mistaken. Markus is at work this afternoon."

Or that was what he'd told me before he left, I was pretty sure. I'd been half asleep at the time.

Nancy blinked her eyes like a big, innocent cartoon character. "Oh... I thought you knew. He's been with me for the last few hours."

My heart cried out at her words. I didn't want to believe her. I couldn't. Not after the night and afternoon we'd shared. Surely, he wouldn't have gone to another woman's house to have more sex?

And there was something about her demeanor, her face... she was gloating. Did that mean she was fabricating a lie, or was she telling the truth and here just to rub it in my face that he'd never be mine?

My brain quickly looked over the facts. She had his credit card... and they were lovers. He'd admitted that already. But he could have left that card at her place anytime. Last week, even.

Something wasn't right about this.

Nancy grinned back at me, and I couldn't stop myself from staring and cataloguing all her perfect features. Her long, glossy hair, her size four body encased in skintight jeans...

I plastered my hospitality fake-ass smile on my face and said, "Well, thanks for that. I'll make sure he gets it."

Then I shut the door in her face.

I leaned against the wooden door, breathing hard. It couldn't be true. It couldn't.

I'm not sure how long I leaned there, but the sound of a key sliding into the door behind my back had me jumping up and moving away from the entrance.

My heart was pounding in my chest, and I was struggling to breathe. I couldn't rein in my feelings of dread and inevitability. I'd told Markus I only wanted him for that one night. That the future didn't matter. But I hadn't meant it!

Could I stay around and watch him with another woman? Many other women?

The door opened, and Ollie's gorgeous smile lit up his face and my heart. "Well, hello, beautiful."

I flew at him, wrapping my arms around his neck and hugging him tight. "I'm so glad you're home."

He chuckled and hugged me back. "So am I! Hey, are you okay?"

I nodded against him but didn't let him go.

"Okay, let me put all this stuff down and we'll go talk."

I managed to pry myself off his stable, rock-hard chest and watched as he put his keys away, shrugged out of his jacket and pulled off his tie. "Okay. Tell me what's happened."

He sat on the couch, and I stood nearby, waving my hands around as I explained that his mom had come by to tell me I wasn't good enough for her sons, then Markus came home and made me feel better, then he'd left, and Nancy came by and said what she'd said.

When I was finally done, Ollie chuckled softly while running a frazzled hand through his hair. "And here I was, thinking you were probably bored from being alone all day and might want to go out for dinner."

At the mention of dinner, my stomach growled. "Yeah... well, I didn't eat lunch, or much at all today, so that would be lovely. But what do I do about the rest of it?"

Ollie held out his hand and dragged me down to sit next to him on the couch. "So... you had sex with Markus on your own?"

I opened my mouth to reply, then realized I may have made a

fatal error there. "Oh my God, I didn't even think about how that might make you feel. That's... I'm so sorry... Is that not allowed?"

Ollie cupped my face with a hand and drew me closer, then kissed my lips. "Hmmm," he hummed, before pulling away again. "Of course, that's okay. It will help you two bond. I was just surprised."

"I was, too," I said, agreeing with him. "You and I get along so easily, it's like we've been together forever. But Markus..."

"It's different. I get it. But you two still click, don't you?"

I didn't want to tell Ollie how hot the session against the wall had truly been. Would he be jealous?

So, I settled for, "Yeah, we click. There's a lot of chemistry, but he's resistant to choosing me. That's why I think he went off with Nancy this afternoon."

Ollie's lips twisted. "You think she was telling the truth? I'll be fucking furious with him if that's the case."

I chewed on my lip and thought about it for a moment. "There was something off about her story. Her tone was strange. I can't explain it."

"But you honestly think my brother would have left here and gone to fuck a chick that he's never wanted? Never really dated. Has always thought of as a booty call and nothing else."

With every word I felt sicker and even worse than before. "You're not making me feel better."

Ollie laughed at that. "That's because you're a woman. And I mean that in the best way possible. Men can separate heart and body. Love and sex."

I pouted. "I know women can do that too." Obviously, Nancy could. "Not me so much, but just saying... it's not just men."

Ollie ran his hand over my leg. "I know. And Nancy is the perfect example. But what I mean to say, is that Markus has never loved any of the women he's been with. To him they're toys... a workout."

"What about with me?" I whispered. It hadn't felt to me like he'd treating our sessions like a workout, or me as a sex toy. The look in his eyes when he stared at me, the soft touches and affection after-wards... none of it felt cold or empty.

Or maybe I was delusional, and I was just another notch on Markus's very notched headboard.

"We'll ask him when he gets home," Ollie said, brushing my hair out of my face and gently tucking it behind my ear.

I loved how affectionate and caring he was all the time.

I stared at him. "How come you're still single when you're so awesome?"

He burst out laughing. "Because I was waiting for you! The woman who was meant for me, who makes my heart pound and my breath catch in my throat."

I leaned forward and kissed him again. "Don't forget to mention the electric buzzing thing. Which, by the way, weirded your mom out. As soon as I told her about you two keeling over, she left."

Ollie's jaw tightened and his lips thinned at the mention of his mother. "I can't believe she came over here and dared to tell you that you're not good enough for us. She's the one who taught us that women are special and should be respected."

I snorted. "Obviously, that doesn't translate to her sons' mate."

"I'll talk to her," Ollie said, "and sort this out. She should have a lot more respect for the Fated mate bond than she's displaying. Makes no sense."

I shrugged and pulled my legs up, curling into a ball and leaning into Ollie's strength. "I didn't tell you. I have some job interviews this week. Not just for hospitality stuff, but assistant work as well."

Ollie wrapped his arms around me. "Sweetheart, I want you to be happy. I don't care if you work or don't work. Or if you want to go study or raise babies for the next twenty years."

"Babies?" I repeated, pulling back to stare up into his face. "I hadn't thought about... you want kids? How many are we talking?"

I also hadn't thought about the fact that I could be pregnant already, not until this moment. Should I go and get a morning after pill?

"As many as you want," Ollie said. "As soon as you can."

No morning after pill then.

"Really? But we've only just met." I couldn't believe that this amazing man wanted to commit to me so strongly after such a short time knowing each other.

A baby would mean a lifelong bond between us. The thought filled me with a mixture of nerves and excitement. Imagine having a baby with Ollie. Or Markus. Or both. They would be wonderful fathers; I could sense that already.

He shrugged. "That's the best part about the Fated mate bond. I don't need to guess whether this is going to work or not. You're meant for me, and I'm meant for you."

I closed my eyes as he lifted my chin and kissed me again.

Ollie tasted of everything good. Sunshine and lazy Sundays. I never wanted him to stop kissing me.

The door opened and a growling, six-foot-three, dark-haired wolf shifter walked in. "That fucking manipulative bitch."

I jumped to my feet, my heart pounding like a steam locomotive against my ribs. "What's happened?"

Was he talking about his mother or Nancy? Or both?

Markus turned to Ollie. "Dad called and asked me to come over."

"Just you?" Ollie asked, his tone indicating that he was surprised.

"Just me," he said, the scowl on his face telling me that wasn't a pleasant thing.

"Uh-oh," Ollie said. "What'd you do wrong?"

"Nothing!" Markus exploded. "They spouted some bullshit about Lexie not being our mate because she's not a wolf. And when I told them they weren't making sense because there are quite a few humans married into our pack, they went on about bloodlines and crap I've never even heard before. I ended up leaving because they were being ridiculous."

"That doesn't sound like them," Ollie said, crossing his arms over his chest in a gesture that looked self-protective. "But then again, neither does the fact that Mom came here to investigate Lexie."

"It was Nancy who told them about me," I said quietly.

"Nancy?" Markus looked over at me, then swallowed hard, his throat working. "When did you see her?"

I hadn't said I'd seen her. Anne had told me. But since he'd brought her up…

"She came by an hour ago to drop this off." I walked over to the hall table where I'd placed the card and handed it to Markus. "She said you left it at her place… today."

I watched Markus's face carefully, looking for clues and to see if he would lie to me or not.

He stared down at the card, then slid it into his pocket. "That's weird. I don't remember dropping it."

I stared at him, dumbfounded. "Did you just admit to going over to Nancy's house this afternoon. After we had sex? You said you were going back to work."

"I went to deal with… Hang on a second." A growl rolled through the room. "What exactly are you accusing me of, Lexie?"

I had the sudden feeling I'd taken a step too far in the wrong direction already, and we'd only just started the conversation.

I swallowed hard, determined to push through my discomfort and confront him about this. "Your mom said that its impossible for you to be monogamous, and Nancy said you went over there this afternoon and slept with her."

Markus's gaze flickered with fury, and the room filled with tension. "I haven't heard a question yet."

Now I was the one getting angry. "Did you?" I put both hands on my hips. "Leave me here just to go and fuck someone else?"

His nostrils flared before his jaw tightened. "You seriously think I'd do that?"

Ollie got up off the couch and came to stand beside me. "Just tell her the truth, Markus."

This time Markus's growl reverberated around the room. It was followed by an eyeroll. "Oh my God, not you, too. Why does everyone think so badly of me? What the hell did I do wrong?"

He hadn't done anything wrong, but… "Did you go over there? If she's lying, just tell me and we can put it aside."

"I went over there," he admitted, and my belly dropped.

I stumbled away, choking on the tears that began welling up.

"But I didn't fuck her!" he growled out.

I didn't know what to believe. "So you just went over for a… what? A chat? Because I know you haven't committed to me, or the triad bond… or whatever you want to call this thing we all have, but…"

Now I was feeling foolish, hoping for love and respect when we barely knew each other. The truth was, I wasn't a proper girlfriend to either of these men. I was a fool, and my heart broke as I faced reality. Everyone was right. Markus wasn't the monogamous type.

"But what?" he demanded. "You assumed I'd be yours from the moment we met? Well, guess what? I have been! I haven't even kissed anyone else since we met."

I pressed my lips together to fight off the tears, finally gathering enough control to speak. "Then what were you doing at her house?"

"Oh my God!" He threw up his hands, swiveled on his heel and opened the front door. "You want me to say that I fucked her? Fine, I fucked her! Are you happy now? You're just like the rest of this town. You all think I'm some sort of good-for-nothing asshole. Well, aren't you lucky that you've got the other half of a perfect pair to love you? Ollie's the perfect part, of course, and then there's me. I'm the one you can just dump because I'm not perfect. Nowhere near it."

The hurt and pain beneath his words were heartbreaking. For the first time I realized he was telling the truth. He hadn't slept with Nancy. She'd lied, and I'd believed her. "Markus… I…"

Before I could get out my apology, he was gone, taking his anger and my heart with him.

CHAPTER 15

MARKUS

The black hole headed my way was huge. And the only way to avoid the depression was to shift and run. Away from town. Away from Ollie. Away from Lexie, and the pain still cascading through me.

I threw my phone and keys into my truck and took off running down our street, breaking into a sweat almost immediately. As soon as I reached the edge of town, I stripped and shifted, bursting into my wolf body and running into the forest.

I couldn't believe my own brother, and the woman who was supposedly my mate, thought so little of me.

What happened to trust? And loyalty? And love?

I'd known what the rest of the world thought about me, but to hear the same bullshit coming from Lexie hurt a lot worse than I thought it would.

I should never have left her this afternoon. Never tried to get that money for her. Never tried to test my own resolve with Nancy. I'd been stupid, and now I was paying the price.

So, can you really blame Lexie for hating you?

I ran like I was being chased by demons, and in a way I was. The only thing was, my demons were inside me and no matter how fast I ran, I couldn't escape their black reach.

The past was coming back to bite me in the ass. I'd just never thought my perfect brother would be on the list of people to despise me.

Lightning flashed above my head and then the skies opened up. Cold rain began to pour down, matching my dark mood. I glanced around, assessing how far I was from home.

Too far to make it back without risk of being struck by lightning.

There was a cave up here in the mountains that my family camped at sometimes, and it would give me shelter until the rain stopped. Not that a bit of water bothered me, but the creek would overflow, and drowning was not on my to-do list today.

I ran hard, around the trees and up the hill, dodging a mudslide and jumping over shrubs and bushes.

When I finally made it to the shelter of the cave, I shook out my fur and walked over to the chest we'd hidden there many years ago. I shifted back to human, shivering in the cold temperature. On opening the chest, I found some old blankets and a sleeping bag we'd left there. A little musty after all this time, but they were dry and would provide some warmth at least.

"Amazing." I would have thought hikers would have ransacked that stuff ages ago.

I began to shake from the cold and the leaching of adrenaline from my system, so decided to set up properly.

I put a blanket on the ground, then climbed into the sleeping bag and sat on the ground with my back against the wall.

I'd finally accepted the fact that Fate might be right, and I might truly have the mate I'd always feared knowing, and yet... once more, my future was totally uncertain.

OLLIE

Lexie wrung her hands and paced the bedroom floor. "Where is he? Do you know where he would have gone?"

I towel dried my freshly showered body. "No idea. Maybe he went to a friend's house."

We ate take-out again because Lexie hadn't wanted to leave the house. She'd wanted to wait for Markus to get back. We called his cell phone, of course, but it had rung out. Then I'd seen it stashed in his truck when I went out to check the vehicle and see if he was sitting out there in the dark.

Either he'd forgotten it when he came home, or he'd put it there on purpose so he could shift and disappear. I didn't mention that possibility. I wasn't sure how she was dealing with the whole wolf shifter thing, and didn't really want to test it out when she was clearly so upset.

"He'll come home when he's calmed down, I'm sure." I tried to speak soothingly. "Shall we go to bed?" I pointed to my large bed that was just beckoning my exhausted body.

I'd had a huge day of stress and multi-million-dollar accounts with problems at work today. I didn't want to talk about it, but I was mentally exhausted.

Lexie looked at me, at the bed, then back to me. "Can we sleep in Markus's bedroom?"

I sighed. "Because it's bigger? I knew I should have gotten the California king." My brother always made the right choices when it came to comfort.

She bit her lip. "No, I just wanna be there in case he comes home."

"He will." I tilted my head at her. "You know this isn't on you. Markus has worried about sharing a mate with me since we were kids. He hated the idea, and it's weird, because he shouldn't have worried. Women have always preferred Markus to me. He's bigger, more confident, and has more muscles."

She smiled. "But you're the sweetheart, and Markus knows that."

I sighed. "Yeah, and despite the fact he makes as much money as I do, he's always been intimidated by the white-collar versus blue-collar thing. And looking back, our parents probably made that worse by commenting about college and education."

Lexie pursed her lips and raised her eyebrows at me. "You think?"

Point taken. "Okay, so my parents are a pain in the ass. I'm not sure how to fix that."

She shrugged. "Depends how much of your life revolves around them."

I thought about the pack and the council meetings, growing up around dozens of cousins and friends. "They're a big part of our lives."

She rubbed her forehead for a moment. "Well, I don't know what that's like. I haven't seen my mom in ten years."

I couldn't even imagine that, and from the look on Lexie's face, she didn't want to talk about it.

"Okay, well then, let's go sleep in Markus's bed. If the big idiot comes back in the middle of the night, at least the sheets will be warm."

Lightning flashed white, light illuminating the windows, and a second later, a great big crash of thunder hit the sky above our house.

Lexie ran over to me. "It's been raining heavily like that for hours. Do you think he's safe?"

I rubbed Lexie's arms and stared out the large bedroom window. "Yeah, of course, he is. If there's anyone in this world who can look after himself, it's Markus."

But I wasn't as certain as I was making out. Markus was upset and liable to do something stupid. He was all heart, even though no one knew that about him. He felt things keenly, more than me sometimes.

And we'd all turned on him. Even me. Shame filled me. Of all people, I should have been the one to support him.

"Let's go to bed." I took her hand and walked her to Markus's room, where the air still smelled like sex.

I smiled as I pulled down the covers and climbed in. "We can never get rid of this bed. It will always be the place we first had sex together."

She laughed at that, crawling into the bed in a white tank top and some underwear.

"What do you think you're doing?" I asked her, mock-frowning.

She stopped crawling halfway to the pillow. "Ah... going to bed."

"Not like that, you're not," I said, pointing at her clothes. "Naked. Please. Now."

She stared at me for a long time. She was probably trying to figure out if I was serious.

And I waited, naked, in bed.

Finally, she crawled back off, pushed her underwear to the floor and pulled her white tank off over her head.

I got a few seconds of perving on her luscious body before she scampered under the covers and cuddled up with me, her ass to my hip.

I rolled over to spoon her, pulling her naked body against mine. "Damn, you're sexy."

She was holding her breath and I wasn't sure why. "You okay?"

"Yeah... um, did you want to have sex again, or..."

I smiled into the dark and pressed a kiss to her ear. "I wish I could, but I've had one hell of a day. Work was insane. How 'bout tomorrow?"

She released her breath in a rush, and I knew I'd said the right thing. "Oh, yeah, definitely. Tomorrow's good."

Lexie fell asleep in my arms, and I lay there in Markus's bed, worried about my big brother and feeling guilty over my role in the pain he was in.

The truth was, part of me had always been jealous of him. Of his easy way with women. His size and strength, confidence and charisma.

But it seemed that beneath it all, Markus hadn't been coping as well as I'd always assumed. And now I just wanted him to come home so I could tell him how sorry I was for not believing in him the way I should have.

CHAPTER 16

OLLIE

I didn't go to work the next day, calling in sick, citing a family emergency. My boss wasn't thrilled, but I didn't give a shit. My brother was more important than any job, let alone one I didn't even enjoy.

Markus and I had always talked about working together. Me overseeing his company and personal finances, and some freelance work on the side. Maybe now was the time to start changing things up.

Only, there was something off in my gut when I thought about Markus. I couldn't explain it, but when Lexie and I woke up this morning and he wasn't back, my worry grew.

Not that either of us had managed much sleep at all.

"Something's wrong. I can feel it," Lexie said in an echo of my own concern. She was audibly shivering even though I had the furnace cranked up.

"The rain's stopped." I glanced out the window and came to a decision. "I'm going to make some phone calls and see if I can find Markus."

"If you can't, we've gotta go find him," Lexie managed to say though her teeth were chattering now.

I glanced at the clock. "It's only noon. He could be sleeping off a hangover somewhere, so how about you go have a hot shower, and I'll see if I can find out where he is."

Lexie nodded and ran up the stairs to the bathroom.

I picked up the phone and called Nancy first. She picked up on the second ring. "Hey, Ollie, what's up?"

"Have you seen Markus today?"

I could almost hear her smirk. "Well, not today, but yesterday..."

"He didn't fuck you, Nancy. *I know.* So, what really happened? Did he reject you? Is that why you came over to our home to stir up shit with our mate?"

The silence on the other end of the line was all I needed. "Oh... you little bitch."

"I'm hanging up."

"Fine," I managed. "But I'm calling my parents as well, and if they haven't seen him, I'm sending out a text for a wolf council meeting."

Nancy groaned on the other end of the line. "Stop being such a drama queen, Ollie. Markus doesn't buy into any of that Fated mate bullshit. And if he's missing, it's because he wants to be. You know what he's like. He's a lone wolf."

I closed my eyes and pressed the palm of my right hand to my forehead. "You don't know anything about him, do you? He's part of a perfect pair, Nancy. A twin. Born to be part of a triad, a large pack. He's anything but a lone wolf. And if something bad has happened to him because you fucked him over with Lexie, you'll regret it. I promise."

In the end I hung up on her. I didn't wait to hear her bullshit response.

The conversation went pretty much the same with my parents, both of them assuming that Markus was just hiding out, shirking his responsibilities of work and his mate.

But I knew my brother. Maybe not perfectly, but better than anyone else.

When Lexie came back downstairs dressed in warm leggings, a turtleneck and a leather jacket, I froze. "Where are you off to?"

She looked dressed for traveling, even wearing sneakers and thick socks.

"I want to go look for Markus. Did you find out anything?"

I shook my head and slid my cell into my back pocket. "No. No one has seen him, and since he left his keys and phone in his truck, I think he's most likely shifted and gone running."

Lexie inhaled sharply. "Okay. Where would he go?"

"The forest. Up into the mountains, probably. There's a cave we used to visit when we were younger. He could be there."

She nodded and zipped up her jacket. "Let's go, then."

I grabbed my keys. "I texted the wolf council and called an emergency meeting. Everyone is meeting at my parents' place within the hour."

Lexie's annoyance was obvious in the twist of her lips. "Why did you do that?"

"Safety in numbers," I said, locking the house and following Lexie to the truck. "We'll be able to cover a lot more ground and track Markus down a lot faster if we put together a search party."

Despite the logical move to involve the wolf council, I was definitely in agreement with Lexie. Something was wrong with my brother. I'd been feeling odd ever since late yesterday, but had put it down to the fact that he was gone, and he was upset.

But even though he was beyond upset at us, I didn't believe he'd leave us hanging like this, with no way to contact him.

I started the truck and Lexie put out a hand. "Can we stop by the drugstore?"

I reversed down our driveway and took off toward town. "Sure, we have time. What do you need?"

"It's not for me," she said, her voice tight, firm. "Markus could be hurt. I want to get anything we might need. Painkillers, Tylenol for a fever. Bandages, first aid tape, bottles of water. Not that I know anything about wolf physiology. Any pointers?"

She was expecting him to be injured too, so I tried not to address our mutual fear, worried it would multiply and consume us both.

Instead, I answered her question as calmly as I could. "We're basically the same as humans. We have a similar life span, but we run a few degrees hotter, and have advanced healing capabilities."

"So, if Markus is hurt... like, he broke a leg or something, he'd heal really fast."

I nodded. "As long as the bone was set right, then, yeah."

She inhaled sharply and nodded, her lips set into a determined, thin line.

When we arrived at the pharmacy, I handed her my credit card and she took it. "I won't be long."

I let her go, because I needed a moment to think. I wanted to shift immediately and head up toward the cave to check it out, but Lexie wouldn't be able to follow in that rough terrain. I needed to clear my head, ready for the council meeting.

When we got to Mom and Dad's house, I wasn't sure how everyone was going to vote or what decisions would be made. But no matter what, I was going after my brother.

Lexie

I had no idea what state we were going to find Markus in, but I could already sense he wasn't going to be healthy. I was practically jumping out of my skin with nerves. I felt... anxious. If I was wrong and he was fine and I'd spent hundreds of dollars on supplies for nothing, then oh, well. We'd have a stocked up first aid kit, which was never a bad thing.

With my pharmacy purchases clutched in my hands, I ran out of the store and jumped into the truck.

"Looks like you got a few things," Ollie said, helping me arrange the bags on the floor so I could actually get in.

"Yeah, well I figured it was better to be safe than sorry."

I'd even bought a fanny pack and a larger bag, in case I needed to travel, though I wasn't sure that would be the case.

"Tell me more about this mountain you think Markus might have run to. Is it far away?"

I was chattering away, and I could hear the nervous tone in my voice, but I couldn't help it. Every time I thought about Markus, I imagined him lying at the bottom of a hill, broken and bleeding, calling my name.

I couldn't stand it and had barely slept last night. I missed my big, gorgeous, tough man.

My cell phone rang, and I scrambled to answer it. "Hello?"

"Hey, Lexie, it's Megan."

Megan worked at the diner. "Hey, hon... we're kinda busy at the moment. I'm sorry, can I call you back later?"

"Oh, yeah. Of course. I just wanted you to tell your friend that the boss won't be in tonight. So if he was planning on coming back, there's no point."

I put Megan on speaker, my stomach twisting hard. "Sorry, Megan, what do you mean? Which friend?"

"Didn't he tell you?" Megan asked. "A hot guy came in yesterday afternoon looking for Geoff. He said he wanted to sort out something to do with you."

I swallowed hard, my gaze catching Ollie's as he glanced over while he drove. "What did this guy look like?"

"Well over six feet. Dark hair, dark eyes. Pretty intimidating."

I put a hand over my mouth to stifle the sob. "When was this, Megan? That was Markus, and we're looking for him, actually."

"Around two, I'd say. I was working the eight till two shift, but Tilly was late, so I was still there."

I inhaled sharply, trying not to cry. "Thanks for letting us know."

"Yeah, of course. No problem. Catch ya later."

She hung up, and tears burned my eyes. "He went to my old job. He was trying to get my money, wasn't he?"

Ollie reached over and squeezed my hand. "Probably. Markus would rather pay his staff than himself, any day. He hates employers who screw over their people."

I nodded, gulping and wiping the tears away. "That's so good of him. I can't believe…"

Did that mean he'd gone to see Nancy after he'd tried to sort out my wages? Why would he do that?

I wasn't going to ask Ollie, because no matter what he said, he was only guessing. I'd wait until we found Markus, then I'd get my answers.

After I begged him to forgive me, of course, because if I wasn't feeling bad enough that I hadn't believed him about Nancy, now I knew he'd been trying to be my knight in shining armor.

I hadn't thought I could feel worse, but it turned out I definitely could.

CHAPTER 17

LEXIE

The wolf pack congregating in Ollie's parents' house was much smaller than I'd expected, but it was a Tuesday afternoon. I had to assume some of them were working and couldn't get away.

"What's this about, Oliver?" a big man asked from the comfort of Anne and David's couch.

We were all crowded around the living room. Nancy was in the corner, keeping her eyes to herself, and Anne was trying not to look at me as well.

Cowards.

I stuck by Ollie's side, not willing to leave him alone for even a moment. What if I looked the wrong way and lost him too? I wasn't sure what I'd do if that happened.

Out of nowhere, those two men had become my whole world, and I couldn't imagine my life going forward without them. As a woman who'd tried never to look more than one day into the future, I now had years mapped out.

For the first time ever, I had plans. I had something to look forward to. A place where I belonged. People who loved me, or at least wanted to build a life together.

I'd finally gotten something worth holding on to, and I wasn't going to lose it. Not now. Not ever.

"Markus is missing," Ollie said, answering the man's question. "I'd like the pack to help me look for him."

The big guy shifted on his chair. "He's only been gone what, a day? Not even twenty-four hours. Surely, it's possible that he's just hunting, or dallying with a shifter from another pack. Markus has been known to do some wild things."

There was a general mumbling of agreement, and Ollie grabbed my hand, pulling me closer. "Markus is my twin, and Lexie is our Fated mate. We know something's wrong with him. We can both feel it."

The big guy on the couch glanced at me, then threw a pointed look at Ollie's parents, then back at me. "Well, no one mentioned that before now. Welcome to the pack, my dear. But I don't see how either of you can feel anything that would make me endanger our pack. You know a storm is predicted for this evening. The forest will flood and trees will come down. People could get hurt."

People? What about Markus? He was still out there.

I kept my mouth shut because I was the outsider and didn't know most of the men and women standing around the room.

"You don't have to force anyone to help us, Alpha. But I'm here to ask for help. If anyone would be willing to search some of the forest with me, we can cover a lot more ground, hopefully getting in and out before the storm hits."

"I'll go," Nancy called out, putting her hand up. "I'll take the north end, near the lake. Markus used to love swimming there."

"Thanks," Ollie said, though I glared at her. She wasn't helping us, she was helping herself. But I wasn't turning away another set of eyes and paws.

"We'll come, of course," Anne said, stepping forward and indicating between herself and her husband. "I suppose we'll go east. Along the city edges and around the forest."

A few of the other shifters offered to accompany Anne and Nancy, and I could see Ollie visibly relax. "Thank you. All of you. And please understand that I don't expect anyone to put themselves at risk. As soon as the weather turns, get home."

The wolf shifters began filing through the doors and walking outside, and Ollie followed, dragging me along.

Once we got outside, I turned to Ollie. "Has someone got a dirt bike I can ride? I'll follow you. I assume we're going up to that cave you were talking about?"

Anne and Nancy turned toward me, the latter with a nasty smirk on her face. "You're going up to the bluff caves, Ollie? You'll be lucky to make it that far before the weather hits."

Ollie shrugged, unbuttoning his shirt and folding it up. "I have to try. If there's anywhere Markus went to wait out the storm, it'll be the cave."

Nancy turned her gaze on me and there was a sneer lifting her upper lip. "You won't make it up there. You're human for one thing, and no bike I know could make it over that terrain. It's steep and hasn't got any roads. You need to be a wolf shifter to travel through the forest."

You wanna bet?

Nancy turned to look at Anne, who was nodding with an oddly triumphant look on her face. Then Anne said, "Nancy's right. You don't belong here, Lexie. Go home... or wherever it is that you sleep."

Fury roared up inside my head. "I *sleep* right beside your sons, Anne. And I suggest you get used to that idea."

Nancy opened her mouth to speak, and I pushed my hand out and snapped at her. "No! You two listen up because it's my time to talk. I've been riding bikes and patching guys up since I learned to walk. I grew up in a motorcycle club and there isn't a bike I can't ride, nor a hill I can't get up. So, you can just shut your faces."

I could feel Ollie beside me, shifting nervously from foot to foot, but I didn't take my eyes off the two women in front of me. It was their fault that Markus was missing, and it was time I put them in their place.

"You better watch who you're talking to," Anne growled at me, the silver of her wolf flashing in her eyes.

I dug deep into that place that was hardened by a childhood that I wouldn't wish on anyone. My man needed me, and no one was leaving me behind.

I stepped forward and glared at the woman who would be my mother-in-law and growled right back.

"Anne, *you* better watch who *you're* talking to. If you don't get your shit together, you won't be seeing any of your grandbabies. And, yes... your son here has made it clear we'll be having kids as soon as possible, so is that what you want? To miss out on seeing them grow up?"

Anne's eyes widened, then her lip quivered as though she hadn't thought about the fact that by ostracizing me, she would lose so much more.

Good.

I turned to Markus's ex-lover. "And Nancy... I don't give a shit if you pull it together or not. I'll be happy to never lay eyes on you again. These men are mine. *Mine.* So get on board, or get the fuck outta my way."

A tough-looking chick with short, spiky hair walked up. "Hey, I've got a bike you can borrow. Not sure it'll get all the way to the cave, but it's the best shot you've got."

I nodded at her, heaving a little from my tirade. "That would be great. I've got a bag in Ollie's truck I need to take."

Ollie grabbed my arm. "I'll shift and follow you. Toni just lives down the road."

The woman, who I assumed was Toni, indicated I should follow her, so I did. I grabbed the stuff out of Ollie's truck that I needed, packing as many of the supplies as I could into the backpack and fanny pack.

"You really think Markus is hurt?" Toni asked.

I nodded. "Yeah, I do. I have this horrible feeling in the pit of my stomach, and it just won't go away."

She walked over to a very nice-looking bike. "Jump on. It'll be faster if we go home on this."

"Hell, yeah," I said, unable to stop myself as I climbed on behind her. "I've missed these machines."

We took off, and just as I was almost enjoying the vibrations beneath me, we pulled into a driveway. The dirt bike Toni had been talking about was in the garage.

"Whoa, that's hot." I said, hurrying over to the motorcycle with huge shocks and a large engine.

"She's full of gas, and helmets are on that wall. Take whatever you want."

I glanced over at the wall Toni was indicating and sighed. "Oh my God. This is awesome."

"You know, I own the only motorcycle shop in town, and I could use some help running the place. What can you do? Mechanic stuff? Sales? Answer phones? Deal with customers?"

I stared at her, shocked that at this horrible moment in time she was offering me something so perfect.

"Ah... I can do it all, really. Got taught how to take a bike apart and put it back together by the time I was twelve. It's been years, but that's not stuff you forget."

"What about the people side of the business?"

I laughed. "I've been waitressing for ten years. Dealing with people and their shit is my job."

Toni grinned. "Then when all this is sorted, how about you come by my shop, and I'll hook you up with a job? Sounds like you're exactly what I need."

I would have hugged her, but a large silver wolf ran up the driveway.

"That's Ollie," Toni said. "I'm gonna shift and join Anne and David. See you later, Lexie."

Toni shifted into a black wolf and took off down the street, a puddle of clothes left in her wake.

I shook myself, still not used to the sight of a human morphing into another creature.

I grabbed a helmet, slid it on and jumped on the huge dirt bike. "You run, I'll follow."

Ollie's wolf nodded, turned tail and took off.

I revved the engine and followed him, and for the first time in my life, I was grateful for the upbringing and knowledge I'd been taught along the way.

CHAPTER 18

LEXIE

Anne and Nancy hadn't been joking about the steepness of the mountain. It was truly one of the hardest rides of my life, but I didn't think of turning back once. We needed to find Markus. My mate was in trouble and I was up to the task.

Ollie took his time on the ascent, sniffing trees and looking for Markus's scent, I assumed. His pace also gave me time to catch up.

Toni's bike was truly fantastic. She'd been right to say it was one of the few machines that would be able to handle this terrain. Some of the inclines were so steep, I had trouble staying on the bike.

Amidst all the worry though, pleasure at being back on a motor-cycle simmered beneath it all. I'd forgotten how much I loved to ride. But the going was hard. I rode through muddy ditches, navigated steep cliffs and slipped between dense foliage.

I kept up with Ollie, though my heart ached with fear for Markus and my arm muscles screamed due to the strain and lack of recent practice.

When the wind began to blow so hard I could barely keep the machine upright, I started to freak out a little. That was the first time I began to doubt whether I had what it took to make it to the cave.

Then the heavens opened up and the only thing I could be grateful for was the helmet visor that kept the rain off my face.

I pushed my fear down. We were almost there. I could feel Markus's need growing the nearer we got to him. We couldn't turn back.

After a particularly steep section, Ollie ran over to me, panting hard. I yelled out to him, screaming over the noise of the storm and the bike. "Keep going! Get us to that cave."

Ollie barked and charged ahead. We kept going and then finally, Ollie pulled up outside the entrance to a cave. Large and black, with sharp, rock edges defining the space.

Relief soared through me. We'd done it! We'd made it.

Please let Markus be here. And please let him be okay.

I dismounted and pushed the bike over a large rock, forcing the machine those few final feet. Then finally, I reached the mouth of the cave.

As soon as I was out of the rain, I parked the bike against the wall at the cave's entrance, and pulled off my helmet. "Markus?" I called out.

Silence answered and my heart sank.

I was soaked, though my leather jacket had luckily kept my upper body a little bit dry.

Ollie shook out his fur coat by the edge of the cave, then shifted back, his human body dripping wet.

He shook his hair and brushed it back off his face. "I'll get dry. You check for Markus."

I unzipped my jacket and pushed it off my body, sweat covering my face.

"Markus?" I called again, this time directing my voice into the depths of the cave.

I couldn't see a thing, and I stupidly hadn't thought to bring a flashlight with me. It wasn't night yet, but with the cloud cover and the rain, it was almost pitch dark inside the space.

I crept forward, blinking my eyes to adjust to the dim light.

I gasped as a man lying in a sleeping bag on the floor became visible. "He's over here!" I called out to Ollie, rushing forward to press my hands to Markus's face. Burning hot. That wasn't good, even if a wolf shifter did run hotter than a human.

Markus was shaking and sweaty, clearly in a fever state.

Ollie came over, wrapped in a blanket. He knelt by his brother's side. "What's wrong with him?" Worry laced his voice.

I had to see Markus better. The bike!

"I'm going to turn the headlight on so I can see him properly. We need to make sure he's not injured."

I raced over to the motorcycle and repositioned it before turning on the ignition and flicking on the headlight.

The whole space was lit up as I grabbed my backpack and rushed back to his side.

"Let's unzip him. I want to check if he's cut or bleeding."

I unzipped the sleeping bag as Markus shuddered, his teeth chattering. "He's got a fever," I said to Ollie. "He's shaking like he's cold, but he's sweating."

Of course, the one thing I didn't buy was a damn thermometer.

I put my hand to his forehead, and he was burning up. "Fuck, that's hot."

I checked over his body and couldn't see any wounds or blood. "Okay. No external injuries. Good. Let's get some water and Tylenol into him."

With Ollie's help, we managed to sit Markus up and force some water and fever-reducing medication down his throat.

I found more blankets and got him out of his soaked sleeping bag, wiped him down with water using the bandages, and wrapped him in blankets again.

When he was as comfortable as I could make him, I walked over to the mouth of the cave and stared out into the forest. The rain was still coming down hard. It was a wall of water, and I found myself grateful for the fact that Markus had chosen somewhere high and dry to hide.

We'd be screwed if we were somewhere low on the mountain.

"What are you thinking?" Ollie asked, walking up beside me, still wrapped in a blanket.

"Ah... just that we're lucky to be so high, really."

Ollie put his arm around me. "You're a true optimist, aren't you?"

I smiled, not able to laugh at a time like this, and cuddled into Ollie's warmth. "I brought my phone. Do you want to call your mom?"

He sighed and kissed the top of my head. "Probably a good idea, if we can get reception. But no one will make it up here tonight. I think we're gonna have to camp out."

"I agree. I'll check out that chest and see what other supplies I can find." I pulled my cell phone out of my fanny pack and handed it to him. "I just wish I'd brought a flashlight."

Ollie took the phone and pointed at the bike still providing the only light in the cave. "Check out the side bags on the bike. Toni's a hiker. She might have some stuff in there."

"Great idea," I said, and walked over to the motorcycle while Ollie texted his family to let them know what we were up to.

"Oh my God, Toni, I love you," I whispered, staring down at the contents of her bags. There was a large flashlight, which I picked up and turned on. "She does pack well."

There were energy bars, packets of candies, bottles of water, a change of clothes and matches.

I turned off the motorbike, not needing the headlight anymore, and Ollie trotted over. "You got everything?"

I ripped open an energy bar and handed it to Ollie, then grabbed one for myself. "Yeah. Eat while I unpack."

The clothes were way too big for me, but fit Ollie enough so he was a bit warmer.

I spread out the extra blankets next to Markus's shaking body. "Let's get some sleep. I'll give him more water through the night." And Tylenol every four hours, if I woke up that often, which I would.

When I pressed my hand to Markus's cheek, he was still warm, but not as hot. "I think he's a little better."

"He's not shaking as much," Ollie said, sitting on the ground beside me and studying his brother. "Come on, sweetheart. Lie down."

"I better take these pants off." They were still super wet and now that I was slowing down, I was cold.

"Please do," Ollie said, a wicked smile in his voice.

I rolled my eyes in the dark, even though he couldn't see it, then peeled the cold leggings down my legs and pushed them to the ground.

My underwear and socks were next, and although I was technically colder now, I'd be better able to warm up out of the wet gear.

My tank top and bra were dry, so I climbed under the blankets with Ollie, shivering hard. "Well, th-th-this is romantic."

He chuckled and rolled on top of me. "I'll warm you up. Just give it a minute."

Ollie was heavy, but I clung to him, loving the reassurance of his body heat and heartbeat against me.

And slowly I began to warm up, the cold seeping out of my bones and letting my muscles relax. Ollie must have felt it because he slid off me, rolled us both toward Markus, and spooned me from behind.

I reached out for Markus, touching his rapidly cooling skin. Relief crashed over me. "You're not allowed to leave me, you understand?" I whispered to Markus. "I need you both."

I rearranged Markus's blankets, shuffled a little closer to him, then fell into a fitful sleep sandwiched between the two precious men.

Every hour I woke to check on Markus, my back aching from the rock mattress we were sleeping on. I force-fed my sick mate more water and Tylenol, praying for the first rays of light to peek over the forest and the rain to ease so we could go home.

But the night stretched seemingly forever, and Markus still didn't wake up, and the rain beat down relentlessly outside, like it would never stop.

CHAPTER 19

MARKUS

Damn... I felt like shit. My tongue was as dry as the desert and my eyes were full of gritty sand. What had I done? Fallen asleep in a kid's playground or something?

Fuck. I had to move. *Shake it off.*

I stretched onto my back, cringing at the pain that shot through my spine as hard, lumpy rock dug into my muscles.

This did *not* feel like a sand pit.

"What the hell..." I shoved the heavy blankets off me. I was way too hot. Since when did I sleep under so many layers?

"Markus? *Markus!*" Lexie landed on top of my chest, her head against my heart.

I wrapped my arms around her, relief that she was here with me flooding over me. "Hey, Lex... whhhy is this mattress soooo uncomfortable? And why can't I open myyyy eyes proppppperly?"

I kissed the top of her head, aware that I sounded intoxicated even though I was sure I hadn't had anything to drink last night. But I was slurring a little, and seriously couldn't get my eyes to open.

She chuckled against my skin. "Sit up. Let's get more water into you."

I wasn't going to argue. I struggled to sit up and managed to crack my eyes open a little. It was light out, just. The red and orange hues of the sunset were just leaking over the trees.

Trees!

My eyes opened wide, but it hurt to do so. "Why are we in the forest?" I glanced around. "And why... oh..." We were in the cave.

It all came flooding back to me. The fight. The rain.

Nancy. Mom. Everyone turning on me.

"Here. Drink this. And eat," Ollie said, pushing a packet of candy into one hand, and a bottle of water into the other.

I tipped my head back and skolled the water, my swollen tongue struggling with the coldness but loving it at the same time.

"Another?" Lexie asked, handing me a second bottle.

I took it but didn't open it yet, assuming there would be limited water and we'd need to share. "Thanks."

I cracked open the packet of candy and shoved a handful into my mouth. I was starving, but had no idea why.

"What happened?" I managed to ask around the candy. "Why are you guys here? Wait." I stared at Lexie. "*How* are you guys here? Ollie I understand, but..."

She grinned at me. "It's a long story. Involves a dirt bike and sheer determination to prove Nancy and your mom wrong."

Ollie stood up from the pile of blankets on the ground and shook his head, walking away. From the line of his back, he seemed annoyed.

Huh?

I glanced over at Lexie. "Any ideas you wanna share?"

"You don't remember shifting and running up here?"

I frowned. "Yeah, kinda. It was raining, and I had to find shelter. Then it's fuzzy. I don't really know what happened after that."

"That was two days ago," Ollie said, glaring at me with his arms folded over his chest. "Do you know how worried we were?"

"Two days!" How could that be right?

Lexie shifted a little closer, pressing a hand to my leg. "When you didn't come home Monday night, Ollie got the pack together for an emergency meeting and we asked for some help finding you."

Ollie snorted out a laugh. "Yeah... and Lexie tore Mom and Nancy a new one when they told her she didn't belong and should leave. You should have seen her."

I glanced over at the beautiful woman sitting next to me. "Really? What did you say to Mom?"

I picked up my second bottle of water and took a sip, waiting for her response.

One side of her lips quirked up in a half smile. "That if she wanted to be a part of her grandbabies' lives, then she better get on board with me being around, because I have no qualms cutting her out, I can tell you. Damn bitch."

I couldn't help it. I spat the water in my mouth out in a spray, but luckily I thought to turn my head in time so it didn't go all over Lexie. "You said *what*?"

"Well, why not? What else have I got to hold over her head?" she asked with a shrug. "Plus, you guys said I'm the one. Ollie reassured me he wants a baby as soon as possible, and you've come in me twice with no protection, so..."

She shrugged like it was a forgone conclusion and I gaped at her, then at Ollie. "You two have been busy."

Ollie glared back. "Well, statistically, you're more likely to be the biological father if she is pregnant, so don't go pretending I'm doing shit behind your back."

I couldn't help but look at Lexie and enjoy the pretty blush that stole over her face. The session we'd had up against the wall had been fucking hot.

"Okay, so, finish the story," I urged, taking another careful sip of water.

"I borrowed a bike from Toni, Ollie shifted, and we came looking for you. Got up here just as the rain came down hard. We found you and you had a fever. We gave you water and Tylenol, and now you're awake."

I glanced from Lexie to Ollie and back again. From the anger-tinged relief I could practically sense radiating off my brother, obviously finding me and helping me through the fever hadn't been the easiest thing for them.

"Thank you," I said, the simple phrase inadequate to describe how I felt that they'd come looking for me. They'd *both* come looking, and had obviously been concerned for my wellbeing. Warmth, unconnected to any fever, lit my body up from within.

But then I realized my body was aching like I'd been training all day and night. "I'm going to stand up. My back—"

"Oh, yeah. Good idea," Lexie said, jumping to her feet.

I was a lot slower than her, not to mention naked. "Damn, I stink." My skin was covered in dried sweat.

Lexie smiled with a cute little crinkle of her nose. "You were sweating a lot."

I stretched out my back, legs and arms, then glanced out the mouth of the cave. "Stopped raining?"

Ollie nodded. "Almost. If we shift and run home, you'll completely heal, and Lexie can follow."

"Sounds like a plan."

Lexie picked up some of the blankets and began to fold them. "Then are we all going to talk?"

Oh, yeah. We needed to clear the air. I hated the tension crackling between the three of us. Anger and hurt on all sides weren't the sort of things that healthy relationships were built upon.

"Yeah. Definitely."

We packed up the cave as best we could, made sure Lexie was safe to ride the motorcycle, then I let my wolf take over my body once more.

It was such a relief to feel my wolf rise up inside me and take over my aching body. The shifter part of me had the ability to heal extremely quickly. I started to trot down the mountain, navigating around the large puddles of water and jumping over rocks.

The more I moved, the less pain I felt.

Lexie was having a harder time than Ollie and me at getting down the mountain. There were no roads, barely even a walking track. How she'd made it up here yesterday, I had no idea.

Respect for her grew, the more I realized how much of risk she'd taken to reach me. We took our time, eventually finding one of the few walking paths where Lexie could speed ahead.

I got up to a gallop, running behind her and loving the stretch and pull in my muscles as everything flowed the way it should once again.

When we finally arrived home, Lexie was already taking off her helmet and parking the bike next to the garage.

Ollie and I waited in wolf form for her to open the door, then realized she didn't know where the spare keys were.

I nudged over a nearby potted plant, exposing the key.

She giggled, snatched it up, and opened the door for us.

We trotted inside and shifted. I cringed at my own smell. I wasn't just covered in sweat. My legs were soaked in dirty water and mud, and the last thing I wanted to do was have an important conversation while I stunk like a stagnant pond.

"I'll jump straight in the shower. Then we can talk."

"I'll join you," Lexie said, walking over to the stairs.

I stopped. "At the same time?"

She shrugged. "Yeah. Do you have another bathroom?"

I glanced over at Ollie. "We need a bigger house."

Ollie's eyebrows rose on his forehead. "You want an excuse to shower separately from our mate?"

I couldn't help the laugh that bubbled in my chest. "No... but I still think we need an upgrade."

Three bedrooms and one bathroom didn't seem enough, especially if my brother was pushing for kids as soon as possible.

Ollie shrugged. "Fair enough. Let's go."

"You coming too?"

He walked up and indicated his muddy legs. "Yeah.?"

I turned away and marched up the stairs. Why was I freaking

out? Ollie and I were twins and had been showering near each other or with each other since we were kids.

I'd hoped for a little bit of peace, but Ollie and Lexie weren't giving it to me today. They probably thought I'd had enough space already.

When I got to the bathroom, I didn't hesitate. I just turned the shower on hot and jumped under the spray before scrubbing at my skin with the soap.

Ollie was already shower ready, but I didn't anticipate Lexie stripping off, then walking into the shower behind me.

"This shower really is big enough for two, isn't it?" she asked, stepping under the water when I moved to the side. "I assumed so, but now I know."

It was a two-person shower, that was true. But the way we were going here, we were going to need a wet room with a four-person shower just to have enough space to move around.

In the next house.

Something about that thought filled me with excitement. I pushed the feeling aside to consider later.

She moved out a little and I ducked under the water, washing away the soap suds and loving the way her hands lingered on my arm, then on my hip, as we brushed against each other.

"I'll get dry and changed," I said as I slid out of her grip and grabbed a towel.

Lexie nodded. "Sure." Then she slipped fully under the water, closing her eyes and wetting her hair with a sigh of obvious bliss.

Ollie turned his back on me to walk into the shower and join Lexie in the steam.

I had to walk away. I wasn't ready to get sucked into playing happy family yet.

Lexie had believed the worst of me. She'd believed Nancy over me. I couldn't think of much worse she could do, other than cheat on us, of course, but I couldn't see Lexie doing that. Especially since it would hurt Ollie too. And surely, she wouldn't want to do that.

Hurt the favorite one.

I reminded myself they had both come looking for me. In fact, Lexie had risked her safety on that dirt bike, and nursed me back to health from what Ollie said.

But the darkness in my mind threatened again. I clenched my jaw and tried to stop my mind from spiraling down into another mess. I'd only just gotten my head around being part of this triad when they'd pulled the rug out from under me with the lack of trust.

I wasn't sure I could do it again. I wanted Lexie, it was true. Since meeting her, every other woman had lost any appeal. But that didn't mean I was going to get suckered into a family I didn't want.

I had a lot to think about before the next conversation, and knowing Lexie, she wouldn't want to wait. She'd want to know how I was feeling right now.

And the darkness inside me dictated that the way I was feeling now was angry.

CHAPTER 20

MARKUS

When Lexie came down the stairs fresh and clean, she was dressed in a pretty top and jeans.

I was in the kitchen, cooking up breakfast. I didn't spend a lot of time in the kitchen. But I could do eggs and bacon, toast and sausage. Protein, carbs and butter.

"Smells great," Lexie said with a grin and sat on a bar stool.

I slid some bacon onto a large platter and pushed a plate toward her. "Help yourself."

Since getting dressed, I'd calmed down enough to focus my nervous energy into cooking. I was starving, and I was sure they were, too.

Ollie came into the kitchen, opened the fridge and started pulling out drinks. Milk. Juice. Iced tea.

I served the last of the eggs and we all sat down at the counter to eat breakfast. The atmosphere was charged but not terrible.

When we were done eating, Ollie cleared away the dishes then indicated the large living room. "Shall we?"

I grabbed a Gatorade from the fridge and went to my usual spot on the couch. I wasn't entirely sure how this conversation was going to go, but my gut twisted up into knots just thinking about it.

Ollie jumped on the end of the sofa, and Lexie perched in the middle, sitting closer to my brother as if seeking his comfort.

Could she really be pregnant already? Was that even possible?

And had Ollie truly told her that he wanted kids as soon as she could pop one out? I knew he wanted a mate and a family, but that would be one hell of a change from our current lifestyle.

"So," Lexie began. "How are you feeling about all this, Markus?"

I raised an eyebrow. "You're going to have to be more specific than that."

She nodded her head and swallowed awkwardly, her lips pulling a little to the side. "About... me. Us. The whole... perfect pair, Fated mate, triad bond."

"Well, aren't you getting up with all the lingo?" I said, shifting to face her properly. "You've only known us a few days, and it's like you've talked wolf all your life."

Her eyes shimmered a little in a vulnerable way before she gulped and said, "Why does that sound like a bad thing when you say it like that?"

Probably because I hadn't meant it as a compliment.

Lexie continued, "I didn't want to believe anything Ollie or you said in the beginning. But seeing your reactions to me... our attraction and chemistry... what your mom and Nancy said and how they responded... How could I not believe in you?"

I moved so that I was leaning forward, my elbows resting on my knees. "Believe in me? You didn't believe me when I told you I didn't fuck Nancy. You didn't believe me when I said I didn't know how I felt about having a mate."

"I did believe that last part!" Lexie declared. "I know you're not sure about me and our future. That's why it was so easy to believe Nancy when she came over and lied about you. And I know she did lie. I know you didn't go over to have sex with her, even though you did go over there. Which still confuses me."

I growled and ran a hand through my hair. Part of the anger I was feeling wasn't directed at Lexie. I knew that. I was angry at myself for being so stupid.

It seemed like I was blaming Lexie one hundred percent, but really, I was angry at me. "You're right. I shouldn't have gone over. It was dumb. I didn't want her. Yet, part of me wanted to know what that felt like."

"What do you mean?" she asked, still sitting on the edge of the sofa, upright and stiff.

I clenched my jaw tight, working through my own feelings of disappointment around what happened. "I mean... I've never felt content. Comfortable. I've always been on the lookout for the next woman. But after you and I were together, I didn't even think about another woman. And when Nancy texted, I wanted to test what my wolf would do. He's never liked her, not really. So I sat outside her place, laughing at myself. I couldn't move. Couldn't even open the door. My whole body locked down. And I... I couldn't believe it. I realized I'd finally found the one. My mate. When I hadn't even been looking, I found you. But then Nancy ran outside before I could drive away, and I thought I owed her a face-to-face explanation about the fact that I was now off the market."

Lexie's eyes changed, her gaze softening, even asher smile sharpened.

Ollie moved around so that he could look at me, and I could see the surprise in his features.

I sighed. "I've never wanted a wife and kids... but I never wanted my own business, and that's turned out great. I never thought we'd buy a house... and we did. So many things in my life that I never planned—or that I thought I didn't want—have been awesome. I wanted to believe this might be the same. But I'm not sure I'm the right one."

"It can be awesome," Lexie whispered.

I shook my head. "No, I'm not sure it can. What if I am what everyone says? A man who can never be satisfied with one partner."

Lexie sniffed and shook herself, then slid a little closer. "Can I ask you a question? Were you happy before? You know... with all the different women. Moving from one to another. Always looking."

I glanced away, ashamed at my answer. "No. There were days I could have walked into traffic and ended it all."

Ollie's swift intake of breath had me flinching away, but when I looked up at him, his expression was sad and reflective rather than angry.

I'd never told my brother about the true nature of the depression I fought on an almost daily basis. The alcohol, women and exercise chased the darkness away, but not for long.

Lexie's hand cupped my face and gently pulled me around until I was facing her again.

She lifted her other hand so that she was soon holding me close. "Then don't you think it's possible that you weren't meant to play the role you fell into? That maybe you've been looking for me, just as Ollie was? Just as I've been looking for you both?"

I swallowed hard, the lump in my throat choking me. "You want a good guy, and I'm not that guy."

She came closer, until she was a hair's breadth away, then she kissed me gently.

I held perfectly still, my wolf howling in my head. He wanted me to grab her and make her mine. Pull her under my body and mate with her.

Here and now.

When she pulled back, she was still smiling. "Did you go down to the diner to sort out my wages?"

I frowned at her. "How do you know about that?"

"Did you stand up to your mother about me and tell her that she was wrong about me not being good enough for you and Ollie?"

I nodded. "Yeah... but what's that got to do with anything?"

She laughed, louder this time. "Markus, you *are* the good guy. You're the action guy. You're my pillar of strength. Why would I ever want you to change?"

I blinked in confusion. "You like that about me?"

"Of course, I do! You defended me! Stood up for me. Protected me. What else could I possibly want?"

I glanced over at my brother, who was smiling softly. "What about Ollie?" I asked.

"What about him?" She looked back at him, then turned her attention to me. "Wasn't the whole point of the perfect pairs to have two perfect guys?"

"I'm not perfect."

"Yes, you are," Lexie said, pressing her hand against my chest, close to my heart. "You're perfect for *me*. I wouldn't change a thing about you, and I am so, so sorry for believing Nancy over you, even for that brief time. It will never happen again. I can promise you that."

Ollie cleared his throat. "Me too, bro," he said softly. "I should have believed you, Markus. I'm sorry."

I stared at them both. *They* were apologizing to *me*?

Happiness welled up, along with a sizeable boost of desire that I'd been trying to keep tamped down since Lexie joined me in the shower.

I grabbed her around the waist and hauled her over until she was sitting on my lap and had her arms around my waist. "So... Mate. You wanna have our babies, do you?"

She nodded enthusiastically. "I do. As long as you two are okay about the fact that I bring nothing to the table. No money. No family. No—"

"Nothing but your own perfection?" I interjected, nuzzling her neck. "Remember that Fate is never wrong about us being perfect for each other."

She gasped and shifted on my lap, rubbing her pussy against my rapidly hardening cock. "Then the answer is definitely yes. I couldn't imagine a better way to begin our lives together."

I moved my hand up under her top, searching for her hot flesh.

"Then lots of amazing sex is on the menu. We'll get you pregnant and start our family. Right, Ollie?"

Ollie got up and walked over to the front door, clicking the lock into place and pulling the blinds. "You're right about us needing a new house, Markus. Something a bit further out, maybe? Big and sprawling. Privacy and space."

I pulled Lexie's top over her head and unclipped her bra, her beautiful breasts spilling out, ready for my eager lips. "Yes, brother. I think we're going to need the privacy."

I turned my mate around and lay her down on the soft carpet, too impatient to take her all the way upstairs to my bedroom.

Ollie walked over, lust darkening his expression. "You guys wanna take this upstairs?"

"Not really." I grinned up at him. I wanted Lexie here and now.

One side of his mouth quirked up in a smile. "I was thinking we could try taking her together. I'd rather have a mattress under her for that."

Interesting.

I stared down at Lexie's gorgeous face, her hair spread out around her like a cloud. "What do you think, sweetheart? Want both of us inside you at once?"

Would she take double penetration tonight? Or would that be something she'd need to work up to?

From the way her eyes widened, I had to assume that was something we'd need to slide into more slowly, sometime in the future.

She swallowed, then said, "I think a bed would be good. Especially after last night on the floor of the cave."

I jumped to my feet, held out my hand and pulled her up. "You're right. Let's go."

I pinched Lexie's luscious ass, making her squeal and giggle, and chased her up the stairs and into my bedroom. The sheets and blankets were rumpled, and I frowned at the mess. "Did you guys sleep in here the other night?"

Lexie nodded, stripping off the rest of her clothes and exposing her gorgeous body to my view. "Yeah… I wanted to be here in case you came home."

I stared at her and couldn't stop the words as they tripped from my lips. I found that I didn't *want* to stop them. "I love you, Lexie."

She rushed forward, grabbed my arms and tilted her head up for a kiss. "Oh… I love you too, Markus. So much."

I crushed her to me, wrapping my arms around her back and tasting her lips in the sweetest kiss I'd ever experienced.

When we broke apart I took the opportunity to get rid of my clothes. I saw that Ollie had already done the same and judging by the state of his erection, he was ready and waiting for Lexie.

But before that happened, *I* needed her. I needed her so fucking bad. The flame of our desire burned between us.

I flipped onto my back, keeping my legs off the end of the bed so that Lexie would be positioned for Ollie to take her ass if she allowed it.

But first… "Come up here and sit on my face, beautiful. I wanna eat your pussy."

She blushed a dark pink, but willingly crawled up my body and threw a leg over my face, kneeling each side of my head and holding onto the headboard to steady herself.

She was amazing, so beautiful and slick, and the delicious scent of her arousal invaded my nostrils. I licked right up her crevice, delighting in the taste, then flicked my tongue over her clit. She bucked and cried out, grabbing onto my hair with one hand and riding my face as I grabbed her ass and buried myself in her pussy.

Damn, she tasted good. So fucking good. My cock throbbed. My need ratcheted up the ladder rungs until I was practically soaring into the clouds.

When she jerked back, gasping and red-faced, I growled at her. "Get on my cock."

She scrambled to do as I demanded, sliding her wet pussy down my belly. Her movements were chaotic, her breathing ragged and indicative of how close she was to losing control.

I grabbed her waist and helped direct her, until she hovered over my ready cock with that wet, slick and oh-so-gorgeous pussy.

"Take me inside you, Mate," I growled, and she let out a groan.

"Oh my God, yes, Markus. Yes!"

She slid straight down onto my ready flesh releasing a whimper as my cock filled her to the brim.

My cock was in heaven. Literal... heaven. Her pussy was wet yet tight, and her channel walls wrapped around me like she had been made just for me. Which, of course, she had been. That fact had never been more apparent than in this moment.

"Oh, Markus, that feels so... good." She moaned and moved a little, undulating her body back and forth, and I almost lost my load right then and there.

"Fuck, I love you, babe," I whispered, shocked at the hoarse sound of my voice. That was what she did to me. Brought me undone. Fully, completely, undone.

My perfect mate.

My Fated love.

The thought gave my heart wings as I reached to cup her face and urge her down to me for a kiss.

Ollie moved in behind her.

"Can you take me here, beautiful?" he asked, and Lexie stilled on top of me.

She turned and looked over her shoulder, before nodding. "I think so. I want to. I want you both."

She turned back to me, leaning over to kiss me again and I clung tightly to her, feeling the rightness of this moment.

Lexie. Alexandria... my queen.

Lexie

Ollie poured some kind of soothing lotion into my seam, before pushing his thumb into my ass, stretching me as I rocked on Markus's cock.

I took his thumb over and over, the soft pain at the start dulling until a strange sense of bliss began to flood over me. I concentrated on Markus beneath me. His strong hands on my waist, his thick cock deep inside of me, his beautiful lips pressed against mine every time I bent forward to reach him.

I put all of my love into the kisses I laid on him. I wanted him to know how much I wanted him. Not just Ollie, but him as well.

Ollie removed his thumb and a strange sense of emptiness filled me. Which was crazy, given Markus filled me with his ready flesh.

But something in me knew, I needed them both. The empty sensation didn't last long. Ollie pressed his lubed cock to my ass and rocked his hips, pushing into me an inch at a time.

It burned, but I wanted it. The pressure. The possession.

I needed both of my mates. Right now.

I began to rock back and forth, up and down on Markus's cock, the movement taking more and more of Ollie until he was fully seated just like Markus.

I was so full and yet, I wanted more. I needed more. I needed everything they had.

"Move," I gasped. "Please."

Markus grabbed my hips, steadying himself and me, and began to thrust frantically up into my pussy, hitting every pleasure point and making stars explode inside my head.

Ollie pulled back and thrust in, over and over, his cock tag-teaming with Markus until I couldn't hold on any longer. I cried out as my orgasm slammed into me, making my belly convulse and my pussy tighten around the cocks inside of me.

Ollie growled and yelled, thrusting once more before filling me with heat.

Markus rode through my orgasm to the other side, then he too met us in perfect bliss, yelling in a strangled tone and coming inside me also in a rush of warmth.

I collapsed on top of Markus as Ollie withdrew and dropped down to the mattress beside us. He reached out a hand and clasped my fingers with his. "I love you, beautiful girl."

"I love you, Ollie," I managed to whisper, though I could barely keep my eyes open. "You too, Markus."

Markus's heart pounded like a drum beneath my ear and I vaguely felt his fingers stroking my cheek, pushing strands of damp hair out of my eyes and caressing my scalp. All I could think was that we were finally together, forging our new future as the perfect pair triad we were always meant to be.

EPILOGUE

LEXIE

1 month later

I grinned with triumph as I stared down at the computer screen in front of me. "Toni! I think we're finally up to date."

Toni stuck her head in the office door and wiped a greasy hand across her forehead. "Great. Now you can come get dirty with me."

I rubbed my hands together. "It's about time."

She rolled her eyes at my enthusiasm and went back to working on the engine she was tuning. I carefully took off my clean white shirt and hung it up behind me on a hanger. I always wore a grey tank top beneath the work shirt so that I could jump in the workshop when we had time. Today I'd be working on an engine.

Life with Markus and Ollie was even more amazing than I'd first thought it would be. Within a few days of Markus recovering from his almost dying experience, he'd gone back to work, bloody stubborn wolf he was.

I hadn't wanted to discourage him, but I was soon bored out of my brains being at home all day without them.

Of course, the guys said I didn't need to work. We had money, they said. But working on bikes was something I'd dreamed of being able to do even when I was a kid. So one day I'd wandered over to Toni's shop, asked if she was serious about me helping out. It had been two weeks since I'd started and I'd never been happier.

The guys were the best thing that had ever happened to me. I had a home. I had men who loved me. Hell... I was eating well, sleeping all night, and was hardly ever stressed. In my wildest dreams I'd never even dared to hope that this could be my life.

Toni had been right about her needing help in her shop. She was always busy with her new bikes to fix, her paperwork was a mess, and her computer files hadn't been updated since she bought the laptop two years ago.

I'd found invoices totaling over ten thousand dollars that had never even been sent to the clients. I printed them and posted them all out last week. Toni thought I was amazing, and even though I had the sneaking suspicion I was already pregnant, she said I could work there as long as I wanted to.

Pregnant. Me! I shook my head and tried not to think about it. Life would change so dramatically if that happened. Ollie and Markus would be thrilled, of course. I already knew that.

I'd learned a lot about wolf shifters in the past month and they were very family orientated. Driven. Loyal. Insane when they were in love.

The sound of a sick, revving engine met my ears and Toni looked up from the concrete where she was literally under an engine. "You got that?"

I nodded and headed for the entrance to the shop, where a girl I'd never seen before was riding a clearly screwed up bike.

"Hey!" I called out, waving at her and pointing to where she could park her bike.

The rider pulled her pink Harley into the spot I indicated and pulled off her silver helmet.

Long dark hair spilled out and the look of annoyance on her face was hard to miss.

"Can I help you?" I asked her, crossing my arms over my chest and smiling at her.

She kicked out the stand and swung her leg off the bike. "I hope you can. I hit something just outside your town, some sort of small... squirrel, or something. Now my bike's not running right."

I squatted down next to the beast of a machine. "Sounds like the carbie's stuffed."

She groaned, pulling off her gloves and unzipping her leather jacket. "Yeah, I know. Fuck it. Just my luck."

I stood up and held out my hand, noting that the woman in front of me was a similar age and weight to me. She'd blend right in. "I'm Lexie."

"Nancy." She said, shaking my hand then shrugging out of the jacket. "I need to be on the road as soon as possible. When can you get this fixed up?"

I glanced back into the shop when Toni was working. Her waiting list was weeks long. "I can't give you a time, but you're in the best place for a bike like this. Come in for a drink, meet Toni the owner, and she can give you an idea of when she can squeeze you in."

Nancy's eyebrows shot up. "This is an all girl mechanic shop?"

I laughed. "Don't think that was Toni's intention... exactly. But she runs everything, and I just came on. So... yeah."

Nancy smiled and seemed to relax in a way that told me she was relieved to know that she wouldn't be dealing with any men.

"It's all good." She agreed. "I just... didn't expect it I guess."

"Come on in." I said, gesturing to her that she should follow me. "You look like you could use a coffee. Or something even stronger."

Nancy chuckled again. "Something stronger. Definitely."

I led her into the office, made her a coffee with a dash of whiskey, while Toni hopped up and went and looked at the bike.

"This is a great place." Nancy said, glancing around at the brick walls, full of bike memorabilia and old posters.

Despite the fact that it wasn't fancy, I agreed with her.

"Yeah, its not modern or anything, but it kinda feels like home doesn't it?" Much like our whole town did.

Toni walked back into the office wiping her hands on an oil rag. "Your transmissions shot, and the carbie's got a hole in it the size of my fist."

Nancy covered her face with her hands. "Oh no."

"I can fix it for you," Toni went on, "Around the jobs I've got booked in, but the main problem is that transmission."

Nancy nodded and dropped her hands away. "I know. You don't have another one, do you?"

Toni shrugged. "It's a custom part. I can order it in, but it'll take a week."

"And money." Nancy added.

"Yep. I'll need the money upfront for the part I'm afraid."

"And it's completely unrideable?" Nancy asked, her tones strained now.

I turned away so I didn't do anything rude, like laugh. It was obvious she was worrying about the money, and I'd been there too many times to think that money worries were funny. But that bike was cactus. She was lucky she'd made it this far.

Toni nodded. "Any further and you'd probably blow the engine completely."

Nancy groaned, stood up and started pacing the room. "Okay.. okay. I can cover the cost of the parts. But I've got nowhere to stay while I'm here."

"You can stay with us if you want." I offered without even thinking first.

She stared at me and I stared back. I wasn't sure why I'd offered, but I wasn't taking it back now. She was a girl alone, and she needed help. Seemed like the right thing to do.

Nancy grimaced at me, "Ah... thanks, but..."

"That's a good idea actually." Toni agreed, interrupting Nancy's speech. "Lexi's place has heaps of spare bedrooms, and her men might look a bit rough, but they're as loyal as the day is long."

Nancy blinked at Toni, then turned to me. "Did she say... men?"

I swallowed hard, still uncomfortable explaining my polyamorous relationship to humans outside of the pack. The wolf families accepted us no problem.

"Ah... yes. I'm in a relationship with two men, Oliver and Markus. We only take up one bedroom, so you could take any of the spares. They won't mind."

In fact, they'd probably tease me about bringing another woman home. They told me all the time that they didn't want anyone but me.

Nancy pressed her lips together, obviously considering her options. Then she nodded slowly. "I appreciate the offer but..."

Toni jumped in again, "The motel's flea bitten and any of the expensive places will be more money than you'll make in a day."

I stared at my boss. Why was she encouraging Nancy to stay with me? It was nice and all, but was there some other reason?

Nancy finally sighed and conceded. "Um... well, I suppose I don't have much of a choice. Ring up the parts you need and take my credit card before I change my mind."

She pulled a card out of the zipper pocket on her pants and handed it to me.

Toni waved her hand to stop the transaction. "I need to make some calls first. See where I can source these parts. How about you go get some lunch and come back. Actually, Lexie, can you go pick up our orders at The Pantry?"

I handed Nancy back her credit card and grabbed my hand bag and a sweater.

"Sure." I said, "Come on Nancy. I'll walk with you."

The biker girl swept her long hair up into a high pony tail. "Okay. Thanks."

We left the shop and she grabbed her cell phone from the saddle bag on the way past. "I can't believe my bad luck." She grumbled, "Seriously."

I shrugged, remembering that feeling oh too well. "At least you're okay. The bike's fixable." Things could always be worse.

"Yeah... but I'm down to my last few grand." She said, staring at the road as we walked along the footpath. "I'll have to get a job here, or something."

"What do you do?" I asked.

She turned towards me with a smile. "I'm a hairdresser actually. Know anyone who needs a cut?"

A hairdresser on those sorts of wheels?

I tilted my head at her. "Seriously?"

She burst out laughing. "Seriously. I just like bikes. Always have."

We'd reached The Pantry and I opened the door for her. "I know the feeling."

Tanner and Wade walked through the door before Nancy could walk around. They were grinning at me. "Thanks, cousin."

I chuckled at the two gorgeous wolf shifters. "Hey guys. I didn't know you were back already."

Wade and Connor travelled all over the state with work and they'd left two weeks ago for some big job.

"Yeah... we, ah... got back today." Tanner said, sounding tongue tied for the first time in his life. He was staring at Nancy like he'd just seen the sun for the first time.

Weird.

I glanced over at Nancy who was avoiding his gaze, then I turned back to Wade.

"Wade... um..." I didn't finish my sentence because Wade wasn't listening to me. He was staring at Nancy like she was the answer to all life's questions.

The realization clunked into place with a thud. *Fated Mates.*

Tanner and Wade were Ollie and Markus's first cousins. They were a perfect pair also. There were a few sets in the pack, but I'd never really taken notice of them before. They were just in-laws, family. I hadn't really considered them single, gorgeous men before now.

There was only one way to find out if I was right about Nancy though.

A shot of excitement shot through me as I said, "Nancy, this is Tanner and Wade. They're cousins to Ollie and Markus. Guys, this is Nancy. She just came into town and she's gonna stay with us for a bit."

I waved my hands between them as introduction, but no one moved. They were all frozen, barely breathing. I was getting a bit excited now.

"Guys, you're being rude." I chided them. "Shake the woman's hand."

Wade glanced at his twin, looking half terrified. Then he lifted his arm, ever so slowly.

Nancy glanced over at me looking just as nervous as Wade was. I elbowed her in the side. "Don't worry. They won't bite." *Not hard, anyway.*

Finally, Nancy reached out to shake Wade's hand and the moment their palms connected, he groaned like someone was pulling his arm out of his socket.

I gasped loudly at the sound. I remembered that noise.

Then Wade collapsed onto his knees.

Nancy pulled her hand out of his grip as she jumped back, rubbing her palm on her leather pants. "He shocked me!"

I'd found a mate for them! How? Why? No idea!

I covered my mouth with my hand as a laugh burst out of me, pure happiness filling up my heart. Ollie and Markus were gonna love this!

Nancy rounded on me with a clearly angry expression. "What the hell is going on here?"

BONUS SCENE

LEXIE

Three years later

My mother-in-law smiled brightly at me as she tucked the twins into the car seats she'd bought just for her car. What a turnaround from when we'd first met. Me standing up to her that day of the wolf council meeting had been the best thing I'd done to shake her out of her narrowmindedness.

She had been begrudging in the beginning, but over time had come to accept me as her sons' true mate. Our children had helped forge a positive bond, of course, and now there was one more on the way.

"Thanks, Anne! I really appreciate you taking them for the night."

"Of course!" Anne said. "You know I'm always happy to have my grandbabies."

I rubbed my huge belly, the baby shifting and kicking hard. "And... if we need you to keep the boys a little longer?"

She glanced down at my belly and smiled. "If you need time to rest or if you go into labor, I'll keep them for a week. You don't need to worry at all. I've got you."

I blinked back tears of gratitude for the woman who'd moved heaven and earth to repair the relationship she'd almost completely shattered.

We'd had several heart-to-heart discussions since then, and when she'd learned more about the upbringing I'd had, she'd opened her arms and pulled me in for a hug. Then she'd told me she would try to be the mother I'd missed out on in my early years.

There had been lots of tears shed on both sides, and now we had a genuine bond that I truly enjoyed.

"I'm not due for a couple of weeks, but I just feel... different."

She nodded with a knowing air. "Kaity was a month early, the little scamp. Always doing things before she was ready."

I chuckled, thinking that sounded like my mates' sister. "She hasn't changed."

"No." Anne waved goodbye and got in the car.

I walked up and blew kisses in the car window. "Be good for Grandma."

"Bye, Mama! Bye!" the twins chorused, waving as Anne drove away.

Nathan and Caleb had just turned two. My perfect pair. Nathan was as light and serious as Caleb was dark and carefree.

Their fathers couldn't be prouder.

And speaking of... Markus's truck pulled into the driveway, and I waved at him, a sharp twang pulling at my lower belly. I stifled a groan.

"Calm down, little girl. You're not quite cooked yet."

I was so excited to be having a baby girl after two rambunctious boys. Not that I should complain. The boys were healthy and strong, and that was the only important thing.

"Hey, beautiful!" Markus called out as he hopped out of his truck and came over to kiss me in greeting.

He had been the model husband and father since the moment he decided he was all-in on this relationship. Ollie, of course, had always been all-in.

"Your mom just picked up the boys, which gives us a couple of days to just chill a little."

Markus laughed. "Chill? You're nesting, big time. What did you start reorganizing today?"

I covered my face with my hands. "The pantry. But it needed a thorough tidying."

Markus pulled me in for another kiss, then grabbed my hand and walked me inside our massive ranch-style home. Five bedrooms, three bathrooms, and sitting on ten acres. It was a dream property, and I still couldn't believe it was ours.

"Well, I've got some of the guys coming out tomorrow to finish putting up the pergola you wanted, and we still need to do some landscaping around the pool."

Ollie had joined Markus's company and taken over all the day-to-day finances, freeing up Markus to do what he did best. Design, implement the projects, and manage people.

They were doing so well, and even though I hadn't been able to work too long at Toni's store because I'd gotten pregnant within a few months, I still stopped by almost every week.

Ollie and Markus had even bought me a bike for my birthday, though I'd rarely ridden it since I had the twins.

Toni and I still got along like a house on fire. She had become my best friend. It was still amazing to me that I had two husbands, two kids with a third on the way, a best friend, and in-laws who had done an about-turn and fully supported me.

Life had completely turned around and it couldn't be better.

"Are you home for the whole day?" I asked Markus as I waddled over to the fridge.

"I have to go back to work, but I missed you. Was hoping I might talk you into coming back to bed with me for an hour or two."

I turned around and stared at him, dumbfounded. "I'm thirty-eight weeks pregnant, hon. Aren't you at all turned off by all this?" I waved to indicate my absolutely ginormous breasts and huge belly, most of which my clothes could barely contain.

Markus and Ollie had been incredible through both of my pregnancies, helping heaps at home, lavishing my body with praise, and hiring a housekeeper when I'd needed more hands and they'd been too busy at work to be home all the time.

Markus chuckled and slid closer. "Are you kidding me? You've never looked more beautiful. And if you take those clothes off, I'll prove it to you."

"Ow!" I bent forward, a large cramp rippling across my belly.

I took a breath, held it, then released it slowly. "Yeah... I think Anne coming to get the boys today was good timing."

Markus rushed over, pressing a hand to my belly. "Our baby girl is on her way?"

"Not right now." I lay my hand over his, loving the way Markus never seemed to stop touching me. "But I'd say it won't be long. Can I take a rain check on that ravishment?"

Markus pressed his lips to my temple. "Absolutely. Though I read that orgasms help get your labor going even faster, so... if you want..."

I shook my head and laughed as Markus pulled me into the bedroom.

Our daughter was born the next day, and a new and even more amazing chapter of our perfect life began.

~

Book 5 in the series, 'Her Pack Mates', can be pre-ordered:
https://books2read.com/u/3JorAX